BETA COLONY

BETA COLONY

ROBERT ENSTROM

DOUBLEDAY & COMPANY, INC.

GARDEN CITY, NEW YORK

1980

All the characters in this book are fictitious,
and any resemblance to actual persons, living or dead,
is purely coincidental.

ISBN: 0-385-14644-2
Library of Congress Catalog Card Number 78-22315
First Edition

CONTENTS

PREFACE

In the year Alpha-0 (the year all modern history begins) a ship departed from the Earth. In eight years the ship reached Alpha and began the construction of a greater civilization than the one that had gone before. Each fifty years after the first landing another ship would come from Earth bringing new knowledge, new people, and a reminder that home and help did exist elsewhere in the Universe.

In the 250th year of the colony no ship came and Earth was silent. Alpha survived and grew, never understanding the Silence or why it had started. In its own time, it too sent forth ships to populate new worlds. But it never forgot its origins and among its earliest efforts was Beta Colony, the attempt to repopulate Earth.

Over a period of 256 years, 2,816 colonists landed in Beta Colony. There are 168 known survivors and/or descendants. Thirty-two of these are in the original area of the island landing site and still reasonably civilized. The rest live in the wilderness portion of the island and have reverted to cannibalism.

"I will cast her off—yes, I will leave her to her fate, unless—"

"Qualify not thy wise and necessary resolution," said Malvoisin; "women are but the toys which amuse our lighter hours —ambition is the serious business of life."

—*Sir Walter Scott*, Ivanhoe

BETA COLONY

PART ONE.

The Island

Chapter 1.

At age twenty-four Daniel Trevor stood in danger of losing his life. If he was aware of this, he gave no sign. Instead, he glanced around the courtroom—first at those closest to him, then at those farther away. In passing, his eyes noted the exits to the room and then paused on a familiar face. A girl's face.

The chains of his leg irons rattled slightly as he shifted position. The armed troopers on each side of him stared fixedly at his face. But he was thinking of something else. His eyes wandered back to the young lady.

His career of crime had been ended by this person in whom he'd placed too much confidence. But he felt no hatred. Perhaps if he had really loved her, he would now be feeling more passion at her betrayal of him. Instead, he simply felt numb. After all, it had been *his* choice to surrender instantly when the state's forces had come for him. He could have fought and died.

He thought of this as he continued to watch with detached alertness. A gavel banged in the background. Massive, heavily padded doors opened and the jury of eleven men and one woman filed in. The judge nodded and one of the jurors fumbled with a small piece of paper. Clearing his throat, the juror read:

"This jury, duly constituted and selected, having been presented with all the evidence, finds the accused, Daniel Trevor, guilty on two counts of the most terrible crime of assassination."

The judge leaned forward. "It is my duty to inform the condemned that, as his crime was most terrible, so must his punishment be.

"As set forth by the law, the condemned is to be allowed the Choice in the manner of his execution."

There followed a long list of sentences that varied in length of time and method of accomplishment but that always resulted in death. When the judge had finished reading he resumed speaking directly to Daniel.

"The Choice was written into the law for good reason. In the early days of Alpha, during the long Silence, religious and other groups were common. Many of these groups placed a great deal of weight on the manner of a criminal member's death. The law recognized the need for this at the time and provided for it. The Choice remains despite the passing away of most of these original groups.

"Most prisoners prefer the quick and painless death caused by the drug MZ 31." For a moment the judge paused. "The law also provides for those who prefer life, any life, to the sentences I have mentioned. At present this alternative would mean taking up permanent residence on Beta Colony."

Having finished, the judge stood abruptly, descended from his high place, and with a swirl of black was gone.

Daniel Trevor sat silently in the tight confines of his "box." He had given himself over to thoughts of the past lately, and now was no exception. He only half heard his state's lawyer speaking from the other side of the glass. Instead, he was remembering the dried-up farm of his youth and the fervent dedication of his father to land that would never yield a fair return for all the backbreak and tears.

"Why?" Daniel had often asked.

"Because this is *my* land!" his father would snarl back. "No one controls *me* when I'm on *my* land!"

And that was one lesson Daniel had taken to heart despite all the other anger and resentment between them. No one had ever controlled *him* once he'd understood what his father had been talking about. And the first to learn it was the man who had taught him.

"Get that seed over here!" his father had ordered.

"I'll get it," he'd snapped back, "but I'll get it only because *I* want to get it."

They stared at each other then, for about a minute, both of them turning slowly red and beginning to steam.

"So," his father said at last. "So," he'd repeated, spitting into the dust, looking straight into Daniel's eyes. "You do just that, son, and we may get along yet."

It was one of the most unexpected things, and Daniel could still remember his own surprise, and he could remember the way his hate for that dry land had begun to falter. It was like seeing something change shape right there in front of him—to know that those hateful rules his father forced at him—to know that the old man would abide 'em himself, and the devil take the first to falter.

Daniel smiled at himself. It was kind of funny thinking of all that hate gone to waste. But then again, he'd become a killer soon enough after that to make up for the waste.

It'd been a strange thing to set him off. Just an article in the dusty old *Argosy News*—weeks old by the time he'd happened to read it.

A Trans-Con passenger shuttle crashed today in the mountains west of here, the article had read. *Suspected crime leader Alpho Dury was aboard, along with two members of the Tang-Signet investigating team. The crash was reportedly the result of an explosion, probably aimed at eliminating Dury and any evidence he might have given to the Tang-Signet investigators. One hundred and seventy-two others were killed in the crash.*

"Now, I hate that." He'd said that right out loud with no one else around, because he'd been eating lunch out in the fields, just reading that paper to relax by. But now he couldn't relax. It wasn't that he hated so many people dying. He hadn't known a single one. It was just that somebody out there had reached out and taken *control* of one hundred and seventy-two people.

Control, in Daniel's mind, was the same as killing. Once something was controlled, it just wasn't *alive* in the same sense anymore. It could just be killed at a whim. Like he and his father controlled the lives of so many chickens.

And now this. It had been like a sick thing to know that dry land and hard work were no guarantees. His father's dream of being a free man was just a bubble of dust. A killer who would kill you for just sitting on the same shuttle as Alpho Dury might just as well take it into his mind to kill a couple of dirt farmers for some other reason.

Daniel shuddered. *Maybe I never should have walked away from the farm like that,* he thought. His father had never even asked why. That was the kind of understanding they had—two men who did and worked at what they wanted, no questions asked or answered.

He'd gone off to become a killer. No accident, no excuse. His only regret being that he'd never found the man who'd brought down that shuttle.

Once he'd tried to explain why he killed—why people who dedicated all of their lives to *controlling* other people needed to be killed. That had been in the early days when he could still feel lonely. But the girl had only looked at him and shrugged. It couldn't have mattered less to her.

Now it was only to himself that he tried to explain.

"Are you sure this is what you want?" his lawyer asked again, breaking in on his thoughts.

"Hm?" Daniel asked, looking through the glass.

"Beta Colony? Are you sure? Once you sign these papers there is no turning back. There is no easy death on Beta Colony."

Daniel Trevor looked at the soft face of the lawyer. "Yes," he said, "I'll be going to Beta Colony."

And even though the lawyer continued to talk, Daniel's thoughts drifted elsewhere. He was a long way from the boy he had been, but the same question still nagged at his mind: How can people want to be controlled? To him, it was the same thing as wanting to be dead. The question haunted him because he couldn't understand why so many had an urge to blend back into oblivion. He was willing to endure anything—to stay alive, even in the hell of Beta Colony—just so that he could go on searching.

The trip through deep space from Daniel's home world of Trent to Beta Colony took seven years. The colony ship was of the latest design and the passengers were awakened only for the final portion of the journey.

Daniel, like all the other prisoners, woke in a solitary cell. The program was simple: Beta Colony was a tough planet. The first efforts to set down a colony had come to nothing. Three hundred years of efforts had come to nothing. The colony ship would offer training to those of the prisoners who wished to prepare for their new home. The training would gradually increase in difficulty until the conditions resembled those on Beta Colony. A prisoner could quit training at any time.

Because of a strange sort of internal logic, Daniel Trevor chose to take his training to the very limits of what the colony ship had to offer. It was the same logic that had led to his instant surrender to the forces of the law. He'd made his choice: He was going to survive on Beta Colony, and until this was accomplished, he'd work at it with single-minded dedication.

It never occurred to him to look at members of the colony ship's crew as enemies—people who were controlling his life. *He* had chosen to surrender to the forces of the law. *He* had chosen to survive on Beta Colony.

His first "training" came in the form of a series of shots and medical treatments that laid him out for three weeks. As he recovered from these, he began an extensive program of physical training designed to restore the body after its long period of cold sleep. Toward the end of the second month, the training suddenly increased in difficulty. For hours on end he was forced to run, and climb up walls and over machines. Without warning, the machines would begin to take part. One by one their great hulks changed into insane, almost comical mockeries of life. One became a groping monster that would flail at him with hundreds of plastic arms whenever he came too close. Another calmly attempted to fall on him every time he passed.

Daniel continued doggedly on, never once tempted by bruises or fatigue to call a halt.

Then there came a distinct change. Attacking machines were replaced by attacking men. The rules of this new game were simple. If he somehow managed to defeat the attack, the crewman was released to try again. But if the attack was successful, Daniel was punished. Aside from the kicking around he got in the process of losing the fight, they gave him an open-handed slap on the face, delivered with an insulting smirk by the man who bested him.

The training was effective. Good as he was, he learned to be better. He didn't lose often, and because of this he was able to last through nine days of the combat.

On the morning of the tenth day he was *unable* to move from his bunk.

After a day of rest and physical examination, Daniel Trevor was led before a ship's officer. The officer's nameplate read "Stassen."

"Mr. Trevor," the colonial officer said slowly, "you are, in the eyes of the law, no longer a criminal. You are now a colonist, and the service you owe the state is to survive on Beta Colony and to improve conditions there and to make survival easier for those who follow you. Do you understand this change in your status?"

"Yes."

"No you don't," Stassen stated flatly. "You're still the same assassin you were on Trent. I don't intend, nor do I think it possible, to change that. My job is simply to see that your natural tendencies are used to insure the success of this colony."

Daniel became more attentive.

"We are seven years from civilization," Stassen continued, "a fourteen-year round trip. Beta Colony's success in the next fifteen years will depend on the crew of this ship and the three hundred colonists aboard her."

"Is there some reason I haven't seen any of these other colonists?" Daniel asked.

Stassen smiled without mirth. "The Colonial Service operates within a strict set of rules; among them is the mandate that we treat *all* colonists as citizen volunteers. We cannot apply force to make you learn. A partial solution is to keep you isolated until you refuse further training. After this meeting you will be allowed to mingle with the others."

Daniel sat quietly for a moment. "I haven't refused further training. I would just as soon continue alone, working with your men."

Stassen looked puzzled for a second. He glanced at Daniel's record. A deadly man. Stassen stared at the calm, tired eyes of a man who had killed sixteen people before being caught at the age of twenty-four. "We have a full library of material available," Stassen said, slowly. "In the two months remaining before landfall the reader in your room will have access."

Daniel nodded.

Stassen hesitated to continue. His whole plan for the colony's success rested on his ability to evaluate the personnel he had to work with.

"There is something else I wish to discuss," Stassen said. "This colony is completely on its own. The ship will stay only as long as it takes to gather fuel for the return trip—and all of that time will be spent in space. It is important to make this colony a functioning organization from the start. Toward that end we've already helped establish a government among your fellow colonists. There might come a time when they could use a man of your skill to maintain order."

Daniel drew in a long breath.

"Yes," Stassen continued hastily, "it may be necessary. Your safety lies in the fact that no one will know you are the executioner. I don't expect you will be called upon more than once, if at all. But we are taking no chances."

"You seem to think the colony more likely to be destroyed from the inside than by the planet," Daniel commented after a moment's thought.

"Exactly," Stassen admitted. "As you may already know, Beta Colony *is* Earth. But it's not the same Earth that colonized Alpha. Whatever malady caused the collapse and the Silence is still at work here. I can only describe it as a sort of infectious apathy. Our colonial structures simply dissolve away with time.

"And partly the problem is that there's no need for an artificial environment, or help from the mother ship. The first four colonies we landed here simply vanished the moment their ship departed. We can only presume that they took to the forests of their own accord and joined the few savage bands that still roam the planet. There was no sign of any struggle.

"Our last three attempts have been made on a desert island, the present site of the colony. At least here we've been able to observe the disintegration. Of the more than a thousand colonists we've landed on the island, only thirty-two remain at the original site. We contacted them by radio just a few days ago. The rest have devolved into savagery, starvation, and worse."

"How can you expect a colony to prosper on a desert island?" Daniel asked. "Aren't you defeating your whole purpose? Forcing them into savagery?"

"Hardly," Stassen disagreed. "All the material needed for survival is provided. However, to prosper and grow, the colony must remain organized and coherent. Without establishing a core of organization here, the colony is of no use to the Colonial Service. Large, unhardened city populations cannot be brought in to a wilderness. Small as it is, this dusty island will eventually be the portal to the rest of Earth. Hopefully, you, the desert environment, the hostile savages—all will provide the stimulus needed to hold this latest batch together."

Daniel considered for a long time. He didn't want this. If he were left alone, he would be glad to build something for himself, and only incidentally for the colony. But it seemed this wasn't to be. They wanted him as part of the team. And what could the team give him? Nothing.

Still, he remained silent.

It was by his silence that he accepted the proposals Stassen made. Daniel would take with him the extra equipment, the detailed instructions on when to use it, all of that stuff—but he reserved in his own mind the final judgment.

Chapter 2.

The ship and landing tractors were over an hour gone and Daniel Trevor was still sweating under the noonday sun. He eyed the pile of equipment, clothes, and condensed rations. He guessed it was about half its original size, certainly not more than half. At least he hoped so. He was tired.

He stopped his work for a moment and watched the two men outlined against the sky. They'd been up there on that ridge watching him for almost an hour. He wondered how long he would have to wait before they paid him a visit.

The hot, still air brought their conversation down to him.

"Let's sit down, Henry. Just watching him makes me sweat."

"You'd think he'd wait till it's cooler to move that stuff."

Daniel continued his work without paying more attention to the two on the hill. He finished moving the last of his six-hundred-odd pounds of supplies into the building that was going to be his home. It was a box about ten feet square, and about three quarters of the floor space was now occupied by his junk. There were three windows, one in each wall, and a doorlike opening in the south wall. No door, just the opening. The windows were fist-sized holes, more to peep through than anything else. Right now they were clogged with spider webs and dust.

On the wall opposite the door there was a ledge. It protruded a few feet from the wall and might have been intended for a bed.

Daniel pounded on a wall cautiously. Streams of dust appeared instantly from between the stonework. Coughing, Daniel concluded that it must be government contract work. The walls were certainly strong enough to hold up the roof—a few shriveled branches crisscrossing ingeniously and sagging down in the middle.

The noon sun blasted through this poor roof and the southern-facing door. The walls and floor seemed to collect and concentrate this incoming heat, and the roof seemed to be trying to hold it in.

Daniel quickly stepped outside into the relative coolness of the open desert. The two men on the hill had moved and were now coming slowly toward him. Both wore crude badges of authority and nameplates on their shirts.

"Can I help you gentlemen?" Daniel asked.

The shorter of the two, with the nameplate "GEORGE," spoke first. "Henry and I have been making the rounds, making sure everyone understands his duties. We think it would be a good idea to form up some sort of patrol to watch out for the cannibals."

Daniel waited for him to go on.

"Well?" George asked, becoming impatient.

"Well, what?" Daniel asked back.

"You trying to be smart?" the man asked. His eyes were contracted with a sort of eagerness, hoping for violence.

"No," Daniel said, "I was just wondering what the question was."

"Are you volunteering for the patrol or not?"

Daniel hesitated a moment, coldly considering the situation. "Sure," he said, "no problem."

"Good," George said, his eyes holding on Daniel. "Henry, take down his name. Give him the midnight shift on the beach and canyon section."

After the name was taken, the short man paused a moment. "We are having an organizational meeting at the Center, five o'clock. Be there."

The two men departed and Daniel watched them until they were out of sight. It was his first taste of Stassen's organized-colony government, and Daniel was not impressed. With so much else to do, however, he simply pushed the matter to the back of his mind.

The walls of his hut, though they were dirty and cracked, turned out to be surprisingly strong—two solid feet of rock and mortar. The windows also presented no problem. He had only the roof and the door to worry about.

He spent the next hour piling rocks into the narrow entrance of his hut. The rocks wouldn't stop anyone, but they would give him a moment's notice and slow down any intruder at the door. Having thus taken his first defensive measure, he separated out and began unpacking the "special equipment" Stassen had provided him with.

It was a 1.1cm rifle (.44-inch), disassembled and packed into an innocent-looking ration box. He assembled and checked the rifle, noticing the bolt action. This limited his rate of fire and was no doubt intended to keep his special power from going to his head. The weapon had good optical and mechanical sights and only two hundred rounds of ammunition. Obviously, he wasn't expected to do any practicing.

Daniel repacked the rifle carefully and placed it along with the ammunition and a few other essential supplies into a knapsack. He was already forming a plan of action separate from the one assigned him. He would wait to see how the colony prospered, but he would be prepared for anything.

He next spent some time rearranging his mountain of supplies. This done, he realized he had only a few swallows left in the gallon canteen with which each colonist had been supplied. He rummaged around until he came up with a small box stamped in red: ATMOSPHERIC STILL: YIELD ONE GALLON PER HOUR AT 30 PER CENT HUMIDITY. In small black lettering he made out the words: "To conserve power discontinue use between the hours of 10:00 A.M. and 6:00 P.M. on clear days. Replace power unit when production falls below one pint per hour during night period. Quality equipment from Dereck and Sons. Distributed on four worlds."

It was nice to know that his life depended on quality equipment.

A few seconds later he watched with satisfaction as the first drops of water forced their way into the collapsed clear plastic container attached to the still. As long as he had power packs he would also have water.

Very carefully, Daniel packed his spare still in the special knapsack he was preparing. The colony itself had a central water source at the north end of the island in the form of a solar-powered seawater-evaporation still. If the one unit he was leaving himself for ordinary use failed, he could always fall back on the colony's central source.

Three hours remained before the meeting. Daniel decided to make use of the time by exploring the vicinity of his hut and learning something about his neighbors. A five-minute walk over a slight rise to the west and he found another building like his own. An elderly gentleman was sitting in the shade of the hut's doorway facing Daniel. The man didn't speak as he approached, so Daniel stopped a few yards short.

"Mind if I sit in the shade with you?" Daniel asked.

"Got some of your own, don't you?" the old man rasped. He didn't sound friendly.

Daniel forced a smile. "That doesn't answer my question."

"Why sure. Go ahead and pull up any ol' rock and enjoy my shade—while it lasts." The old man spat on the ground after speaking.

"While it lasts? What is that supposed to mean?"

The old man's lips cracked into an ugly smile. "You new folks, not too fast on the uptake. Well, it doesn't matter much." He chuckled softly to himself. "My old bones won't tempt 'em much anyway. Already rejected me twice. An' now they got young stuff to choose from."

Daniel didn't know what to say. The old man was obviously used to talking to himself. "Haven't they told you about the patrol yet? The savages won't be able to get by it."

The old man really laughed this time. He rolled in the dirt, kicking his feet in the air. Finally he gained control of himself. "Think you're smart. Patrol! Hah," he spat again. "Wait'n till they start takin' you, one by one, week by week. Then come'n tell me 'bout your patrol. Hah!"

Daniel shook his head and turned away. Walking up the slope he heard the old man shout something after him but he didn't listen. The old man was obviously one of the old colonists Stassen had told him about—half crazy with fear and a broken and useless man. Daniel didn't look forward to meeting any more of them.

He didn't stop walking until he was back at his own place. He rested a few minutes in the shade, then started toward the east. The closest hut in that direction was a little farther away than the old man's. It no sooner came into sight than a burst of noise hit him. He stopped. The noise was coming from the hut and he could tell that there were two people making it. A man and a woman screaming at each other.

He started to turn away when the woman stumbled out. She was laughing and panting for breath. She cried out in delight when she saw him, then ran around the corner of her building and out of sight. She shouted at the man inside.

"Hey, big man, you got some competition out here!"

The man emerged wiping his face. It was Henry, one of the badge-wearing symbols of authority he'd met earlier. Henry squinted his eyes against the sun. He scanned the horizon like slow-moving radar.

When he caught sight of Daniel he shifted position to face him. He tried to shade his eyes against the sun to see who it was.

"Is that you, George? I know I shouldn't be here, but—" He sounded frightened.

The woman laughed from behind the building. "What's wrong, *Henry?* Someone you can't handle?"

"Shut up!" Henry shouted. He was beginning to suspect that he wasn't talking to his brother George after all. He came up the hill for a closer look. "You!" There was obvious relief in his voice. "Beat it." He turned his back contemptuously and started back down the hill and around the building.

Daniel shrugged and started back toward his own hut. The quality of the colonists he'd found so far didn't seem too good. More and more he found the solitary urge growing in him. He didn't like people in general. Why should he exert himself for this hash of criminals when they had obviously been abandoned to die on this baking island?

The meeting began at five o'clock in the afternoon, exactly. Ralph Randolph, the eldest of the three brothers running the colony, was the sole speaker. Unlike his brothers, George and Henry, he was a thin, serious-looking man. He explained the water situation briefly and assigned several men to guard and supervise the central still at the north end of the island. He also explained the supply and the food situations. Enough condensed rations had been landed at the central warehouse for ten years of careful eating for the entire colony. Each colonist also had a six-month supply at his or her hut. Colonists were to remain unarmed until conditions warranted otherwise. Members of his personal security force would be armed with a sort of long knife and a two-foot long club. These two weapons would also be issued to border-patrol people while they were on active duty. The initial border was located about three miles from the northern tip of the island and would be patrolled constantly until the nature, strength, and intent of the savages living in the South was determined.

Ralph Randolph finished by saying, "The survival of this colony and all of us depends on following orders and hard work. Tomorrow I expect everyone to spend the day exploring our part of the island and relaxing. The day after, you will each be assigned work duties that will keep you too busy for this kind of activity. Assemble here promptly at 8:00 A.M. day after tomorrow."

It was as Ralph Randolph concluded speaking that a disturbance took place at the rear of the assemblage. The agitation spread rapidly and soon people were departing in anger toward their huts. It was some time before Ralph Randolph learned the nature of the rumor that had caused this sudden dispersal. Someone had apparently whispered that the Randolphs might have been out collecting taxes from the colonists' private supplies while the meeting was going on. While no one had made this charge openly, they had all gone off quickly enough to check it.

This hint of a possible troublemaker caused Ralph Randolph some concern and he immediately began questioning members of his security force, trying to discover the source of the rumor. He would have been shocked to learn that he himself and the troublemaker were already the subjects of close observation by the much-maligned savage residents of the southern half of the island.

Hot air blew against the bony ridge of the island. Concealed among the rocks lay two figures browned by years of sun and exposure.

Derbid brushed back the hair from his eyes with a hand calloused by work and age. From his hiding place he could see most of the island to the north and west of him. Heat shimmered from the ground and there was still a burning strength in the sun, just two hours from setting.

The great ship had come and gone long hours ago and Derbid had been watching the new colonists ever since. They had gathered in the crude amphitheater almost directly below him and he watched with great interest as their meeting began.

Never before had he seen so many. Three times in his life he had watched the great ships come, but never before had one left so many. He watched with special attention the man who stood in the center and did all the talking. It was important that Derbid locate this man's dwelling place. Looking through the long sight, he could see the man's face clearly. Derbid memorized it.

He motioned behind him for his daughter to come forward. She came, crouching low, without a sound. He pointed at the man speaking. "Listen to him," he commanded, pushing her back from the edge of rock after she had seen the man he pointed out. "You must tell me what that man is saying."

The girl's eyes flared briefly in anger. She was barely fifteen years of age and this was the first landing she had seen. She wanted freedom to seek among the assembled minds as she chose, following her own curiosity. But instead, she submitted, doing as her father commanded.

Clearing pebbles and thorns from a level space of ground, she lay down on her stomach, resting the side of her head on the backs of her hands. The burning heat of the ground seemed only to relax her, and her eyes closed. Soon she was mumbling, repeating the far-off words of Ralph Randolph as he spoke them—long before the sound could have reached her. Derbid listened closely to the mumblings of his daughter and kept his eyes on the distant speaker.

Derbid was very hungry. He was glad the ship had come again and that more people were here to bargain with. They looked very strong and healthy. The creature of the Flame would be satisfied with them. Food and wealth would be assured to the community for a long time to come. And to his family as well, for the strength of his far sight and the gift of his daughter's listening would again earn him position and reward.

The talk was ending and Derbid was glad of the wealth of these new people and their weakness of weapons and scant knowledge of the island. He was also glad that they had strong leadership. Thus he would have to deal with only the one man and not with a multitude of independent spirits.

It was at this point that a disturbance rocked the meeting. Derbid's eye was upon the source of this problem immediately. He memorized the face he saw. Impatiently he nudged his daughter from her seeming slumber and pointed out this new man to her. "Follow," he ordered. "Listen to him and if he is a threat to this leadership, kill him."

His daughter obeyed silently. She disappeared behind the rocks of the ridge and began following the prey her father had pointed out.

Returning his attention to the leader, Derbid saw that he was engaged in heated discussion with others of his following. Derbid kept only half his mind on them, however. In his heart he felt troubled. This group was not the same as all the others. They had followed a single leader too soon. It caused him to think troubled thoughts.

In the coming night he would discover if his troubled thoughts were justified.

The secret ledge was never wider than five feet. Before Derbid had discovered it, it had been covered with the rubble of time, fallen from the cliffs above it. The ledge was there because worms had once wormed their way through a dense layer of mud. The worms had died, leaving behind them a layer of mud honeycombed with holes. Dissolved minerals had filled those holes and hardened with time. And now, high above the sea that had formed them, one layer of the sandstone cliffs resisted the weather a little more than its fellow layers. Derbid and the community didn't know about the dead worms, or the work they had done. But they did know of the ledge and without it Derbid and all of the community would have long since grown thin with hunger.

Derbid moved along the ledge, and two hundred feet below, the angry surf crashed in its endless war against the rocks. Two hundred feet above him the newly arrived colonists slept in peace and false security. A few of the new colonists watched to the southeast and marched uselessly along their patrol line. Some watched elsewhere, but none watched over the four-hundred-foot cliff, which dropped straight into the sea along the island's entire eastern edge. No one watched at the north end of the island where the four-hundred-foot cliff shrank gradually to nothing, and where a wormy layer of sandstone became an eroded mesa covered with stone huts and sleeping people.

Just before the small ledge broadened into a mesa there was a break. A recent slide had taken out a twenty-yard section of the ledge and left in its place a gaping chasm. But this slide had also exposed strong and unweathered rock, rock that afforded finger- and toeholds that didn't crumble away when you put your weight on them.

Derbid scrambled up this vertical pathway, and three others followed him. Twenty feet they climbed, then emerged silently upon the edge of a moonlit tableland. The land sank gradually away in front of them and they paused to overlook it and wait for the moon to sink into and below the western sea.

When it was gone, they traveled quietly along well-remembered paths and finally stopped before one of the huts that dotted the mesa.

Derbid pointed at the hut and spoke in low tones with the three men who accompanied him.

A dim light burned inside the building and they could see a guard slumbering, propped against the entrance. The four men crept closer. Derbid looked closely at the sleeping man. It was not the leader they were seeking and he shook his head negatively to tell the others so. Thus the sleeping guard was killed quietly as they entered the building. Derbid stood to one side and let the leaders of his community do their work.

Ralph Randolph woke with a start. Something hard and sharp was pressed against his throat. He waited a moment to die and when he didn't, he opened his eyes. A pair of sun-browned and bearded faces looked down at him. Another stood in the shadows by the door, and a fourth was making himself comfortable on a pile of supplies. For a moment Ralph looked around wildly for help, then he subsided when he saw that both his brothers were sprawled unconscious on the floor.

"My name is Grant," the man sitting on his supplies said. "I am the leader of my community. These are my two sons. We have come to welcome you to our island. What is your name, and the names of these two?"

"Ralph Randolph, and those are my brothers, George and Henry."

The sitting man leaned closer. "You will speak more quietly, please."

Ralph swallowed and nodded.

The pressure of the knife against his neck relaxed a little.

Grant spoke again. "Perhaps you will be more careful from now on? A leader like yourself should not die at the hands of savages. If you are smart you will learn from this experience. Do you know what you will learn?"

Ralph was baffled by this line of questioning. He looked toward the doorway. "Ah, perhaps two guards?" He smiled tentatively at this suggestion.

Grant laughed. "I like you, Ralph. You are a funny man. A smart man too." He leaned closer and breathed into Ralph's face. "You will learn that we can come and kill you any time we want. And from this, you will learn that you must co-operate with us. Do you understand that?"

Ralph looked frankly into the savage's eyes. "Yes. I understand you."

"Good. Every night you will continue your patrols and the appearance of defense. Every ten days you must bring us one person. He must be living and in good health. No sickness! Make sure no one knows what you are doing. If you do this you will be able to keep everything that belongs to that person and we will not come to kill you. This way both our peoples will live in plenty. Otherwise you would soon run out of food and die of starvation anyway. It is a good arrangement for both of us."

"Yes," Ralph answered calmly, "I think it is a very good idea."

"All you have to do," Grant continued, "is escort them up the main trail to the South—toward the top of the island. We will do the rest and we will inform you of when we want the first one."

Standing in the darkened corner where he had been listening, Derbid shook his head. It had been easy after all.

Chapter 3.

Daniel Trevor felt no pride. He had caused the trouble as a calculated act. The Randolph government was a one-man dictatorship. By starting the rumor about secret tax collections, he had set a bound beyond which the dictatorship could not go. Colonists now considered their first lump of supplies and equipment as personal property. They would resist the government with possessiveness and indirectly protect *him*. He didn't want anyone touching his stuff—especially when snooping might uncover his special equipment.

In a number of ways Daniel was actually impressed by the system of the Randolph government. In less than a day on the ground they'd already established a patrol line, and he was one of the "volunteers" presently walking this line.

Aside from the obvious danger that the solitary patrollers faced, Daniel found himself enjoying his job. He'd drawn the beach section of the line, about half a mile in length and mostly level. Only in the last part did it rise abruptly from the sand to meet on higher ground with the next volunteer's section.

The cool air and soft sand were treats. The moon made the use of his flashlight unnecessary. He could check the beach for footprints and that was just about all he was required to do. He wasn't expected to fight off a hostile invasion with the club and knife they'd given him, just give a warning. He had a small metal bell, wrapped to keep it quiet, and this was his most important tool.

A very simple system. It might even work. Daniel smiled at the thought. He could hardly believe a real threat existed. Savage cannibals! It smelled too much like a device to keep the real savages he'd come down with from tearing each other apart.

Daniel laughed quietly to himself. Then a shift of the wind brought a faint odor to his nostrils. He dropped to the ground and lay motionless. He closed his eyes and concentrated a moment. The smell itself was not what he feared. There was something else. A feeling of constriction—like a bag of darkness trying to squeeze away his life. It was not a new feeling, but always before it had only come when his life indeed was about to end.

A cold sweat sprang out on his upper lip. He crawled slowly to one side, into the partial shelter of a beach dune. He made no noise. Even the sound of his own breathing was covered by the pounding of the surf. Slowly he slipped the two-foot polished wood club into his right hand. The knife he left where it was. The blade would flash in the moonlight.

The only sign he had to go by was wind direction and that one brief whiff of dry sweat and cooking grease. Rather than wait, Daniel surged forward in a swift glide over the swell of his dune. As he did so, the bag of darkness seemed to rip and shred away with each step.

As he ran, Daniel scooped up sand in his free hand. But already his fear was draining away. He slowed to a stop. Was he chasing the shadows of his own mind? But there had been a smell of something.

He moved forward a few more paces. A withered bush protruded from the sand. Behind it were soft indentations in the sand. Something—perhaps an animal—had rested here for a few moments, or perhaps it had scratched in the sand for some grubby worms to eat.

Daniel checked the ground carefully, but the sand was too dry and the indentations too blurred to identify. They were small. The size a child or medium-size animal might make. It was a puzzle. Never before had he felt so let down. The danger *had* been real. He trusted his own feelings to that extent. But there was nothing here—nothing he could sink his club into or batter out of existence.

He backed slowly, scanning the beach line and tangle of dunes. Nothing moved. He turned at last and jogged back to the patrol line. He was well behind schedule now and didn't want to cause a commotion by showing up late at his rendezvous.

The moon was now gone, sunk in the ocean, and for the first time he was forced to use his light to check the sand for prints and to keep from stumbling on the rockier portion of his trail. He moved slowly despite his need to hurry. There were sharp gullies in this last several hundred yards and they were just deep enough to conceal a man or break a careless leg.

As he worked his way higher, the sound of angry voices drifted down to him. Daniel shut off his light and moved off the trail. The voices came closer and he was taking no more chances on this night.

Lights appeared in the distance, wavering faintly. The voices began to make sense and Daniel listened carefully.

"No!" one of them said.

"Are you sure?"

"Damn it, patrol these rocks yourself if you want to be so sure! I didn't ask for this job."

"Watch your step, Dillon. I'm in no mood for an argument tonight."

There was silence for a few seconds, then the lights stopped moving.

"This is the end of my patrol area. Take a look around. Can *you* see anything? Can *you* hear anything?" There was no audible reply. "I didn't think so. Well, it's four and I'm off. If you want to continue the discussion you know where to find me."

One of the lights started back up the trail. The other three stayed. For several minutes Daniel waited but they didn't seem inclined to move. He decided he'd better reveal himself. As he stood up all three lights turned toward him and he covered his eyes, momentarily blinded.

"Please lower your lights."

The lights stayed on his face.

"Suit yourselves," he said and shrugged.

"Caught you napping, didn't we?" The voice of George Randolph was filled with hate as he moved forward and kicked out with his right leg.

Daniel stepped aside. He caught the leg under his left arm and poked his club into the man's stomach. He did this without force, but held the leg and club so that George Randolph was helplessly held off balance on one foot.

The man's teeth made a grating sound. "Damn you! Let go. You sleeping dog. You're going to pay for letting them through."

Daniel let go of the leg and pushed, sending George back into the waiting arms of his brother.

"I haven't been sleeping," Daniel said gently.

George struggled to attack, but he was restrained.

"Ease off, George." Ralph Randolph's voice was without emotion. Commanding. "The man is telling the truth." He didn't mention the fact that Dillon's report already made this obvious. Ralph was aware that his brother was suffering from a severe blow to the head, and thus Ralph made allowances. "Anything unusual happen along your line tonight, Trevor?"

Daniel paused for a moment. "Thought I saw something once, but nothing came of it."

"No one crossed your patrol line?" Ralph asked.

"Not a living soul."

"Hope you're right, Trevor. We'll check for prints just the same. We brought your replacement along so you can go now."

The three started down the line and Daniel watched them go with mixed feelings. Until a few minutes ago he hadn't been worried about any other one person on the island. Now he didn't feel quite so confident.

Ralph Randolph was not simply the acting head of the colony government, he also was a man who knew what he was doing.

Daniel wondered what had happened to bring the brains of the Randolph government out at this time of night. Daniel also wondered if Ralph knew about his role as the government's assassin. It would explain why he had been so quick to restrain his brother.

Daniel thought about this as he walked back toward his hut. Some penetration had obviously been made by the savages, and this probably meant a further strengthening of the patrol line. Tonight, he decided, was the night to hide his emergency supplies. If he waited he might not get another chance.

His knowledge of the patrol line made this easier. He carried the heavy pack he'd made up and crossed the line at a point where he knew no prints would be left.

He traveled about a mile and a half into savage territory, turned up a small canyon, and buried the pack partway up a small cliff. He studied the location and its surroundings carefully, memorizing the slopes and landmarks that would make finding the pack again possible.

Daniel was careful to step on rock or very soft sand, leaving little trace of his coming and going.

The first light of false dawn was glowing in the sky as Daniel returned to the patrol line. He found to his dismay that the ground where he had originally crossed the line had been covered with a white powder—chalk or flour—which must have been brought up from the main supply depot during the short time he'd been gone. All the rocky or hard-pan parts of the line were now covered with this powder.

How was he going to get across without leaving a trace? Daniel thought furiously for a moment, then flattened into the ground as his replacement on patrol approached. Daniel waited breathless until the man was gone. The beach was Daniel's only chance.

He backed off from the line, hurried down a depression in the beach dunes, and waded out until the water was up to his neck. Gentle swells would lift him off his feet, but between them he would walk northward as rapidly as possible. Real dawn was breaking as he struggled out of the water far to the north of the patrol line. He was safely back in his hut long before the colony began coming to life.

He went to sleep secure and gratefully fatigued. . . .

Derl, daughter of Derbid, ears of the island community, listened. She pressed her body deeper into the soft sand. The man she followed returned, his actions strange in trying to hide from his own people. He almost stepped on her as he came by, hurrying to the water's edge and wading in. She did not move, frightened by the strangeness of this man and her inability to listen.

His mind was a blank—a polished and cold nothing. She heard no thoughts, no emotion, no beatings and murmurings of body language. Nothing.

Because of this Derl had failed. The man was still alive. Failure made her cringe and shiver. There was no excuse for failure. Her father would beat her and withhold food. She would be shamed before the community and revenged upon by all the children and young people who feared and hated her for her power to listen.

What could she do? How could she avoid this hateful punishment? Her mind raced upon the possible paths of escape and always it came back to the glaring eyes and snarling anger of her father. He hated her—he liked to punish her. But also, he liked to use her power, to make others frightened of him and hateful of her.

How could she escape? What could she do? . . .

It was a strange sickness. None of the new colonists were immune. Between three and six days after their landing everyone contracted the disease. A few died, but most recovered rapidly two days after the first symptoms appeared. Fortunately it did not strike everyone simultaneously. Most of the old colonists had already lived through several waves of this sickness and they were only slightly affected by the new outbreak.

As in the past, the older colonists tried to make use of the sickness around them as a time for looting and restocking their supplies from the larders of their newly arrived brethren. Three of the older colonists died finding out that things were different this time. No looting was permitted by the Randolphs.

For Daniel the sickness was a new and unpleasant experience. Aside from the artificial illness on the ship, he'd never been sick in his life. Sickness was a rare thing on Trent, something that only struck the weakest. But this sickness was different. It was Earth-born and it struck its returning hosts hard.

The strength left Daniel's legs and he couldn't eat. His vision blurred whenever he tried to move and his mind was foggy all the time. He had trouble performing the simplest tasks.

In the second day of his misery, at the height of the sickness, he had a visitor. He heard the tumbling of rocks at his doorway and struggled to sit up—to make some defense. "What do you want?" he whispered to the dark shape leaning over him.

"Just relax," his visitor spoke. It was Ralph Randolph. "I came to talk." Nodding toward the rocks piled in the doorway, Randolph added, "That's not a bad idea. Could have used it myself a few days ago when we had visitors."

"No use now," Daniel managed to say.

"Yes, I can see that. You really don't look too good, but you'd better get well fast. You're leaving tonight."

Daniel tried to speak but Randolph quieted him with a hand. "There isn't much time to explain," Randolph continued. "I know what you are in the plan of things and that is why I'm going to the trouble of keeping you alive. Until we establish adequate security on this hellhole I've got to bow to the natives' wishes, and they want you. And that means I've got to keep you alive and give in to them at the same time."

Daniel tried to understand this and to say something, but his mouth felt dry and gummed closed. He had trouble keeping his eyes open. He began to see things. He wasn't sure if they were real.

The crazy old man's face seemed to be floating in front of him and laughing.

"Be careful with him," he heard Randolph's voice ordering the old man. Then closer, whispering in his ear, Randolph's voice was explaining, "They're demanding you be sent to them as soon as you're well, which is tomorrow by their calculations. But if you are not here, then I can't send you to them. So you are going to get well early and leave before we come to get you. The old man here is going to carry you out and hide you with some supplies. In return, he'll get what we have to leave behind."

Daniel didn't remember much after that, except being vaguely surprised by the old man's strength.

It was dark and Daniel was carried none too gently about half a mile past the patrol line and dumped unceremoniously among some bushes. The old man stopped just long enough to murmur something in his ear.

"Poor Ralph," the old man said, "he got a little sick back there, couldn't come all the way with us. Had to go back. Heh. Heh." The old man laughed dryly, with no humor.

"Now, you won't be needing all these nice supplies, will you? Oh that's nice. Didn't think you really wanted them. I'll just take 'em back with me.

"Now, you just rest quiet here for a while." The old man stood up as he spoke and kicked Daniel in the side. "There, now I've made you real comfy and I've got to be going." The old man chuckled and disappeared into the darkness.

When Daniel woke the sickness was gone. He was laying face down in the sand with one arm pinned under him. He rolled over and sharp pains worked their way up and down his arm. He waited, gasping, as the blue tint slowly drained from his arm and the pain subsided a little.

Gingerly, he rubbed small sharp bits of gravel from indentations in his arm. They left small white pockmarks, which were slow in disappearing.

Daniel sat up slowly. The blazing heat of near noon was all around. He should have been dead. He was going to be dead. In this heat he should never have awakened.

He turned slowly to look around. The back of his neck screamed with pain, and several sunburn blisters burst, sending dribbles of liquid down his back and under his shirt. For a moment his mind blurred with pain and he almost passed out.

The sun was high, driving toward noon, and the burns on the back of his neck convinced him that he had to find shade quickly. He couldn't walk. The bottoms of his feet and the backs of his legs almost up to his knees were covered with the same burns and blisters as his neck.

He had no water, no food, and almost no strength. The sea was to the west, the colony to the north, and meat-eating savages in the other two directions.

Daniel scanned the hills to the east with the beginnings of panic. He had to find the dry creek where he'd hidden his emergency supplies. He began to crawl. The sand was soft but burning hot. Much hotter than the air. The sand ended and griddle-hot rocks burned at his knees despite the padding he tried to protect them with.

He collapsed into the shade of a twisted bush, which somehow held leaves enough to shade him. Instantly a throng of vigorous insects attacked, defending the nest he'd fallen on. He rolled away, fortunate to find a nearby bush unclaimed. He rested in the shade. He couldn't keep this up. His knees were bleeding now and his hands were raw from crawling.

Slowly his normal calm returned. He had no map with him, but he remembered crossing only two creekbeds between the patrol line and the canyon where he'd hidden his cache. It couldn't be too far away. He relaxed, deciding to wait for darkness and save what strength he did have.

While he waited he broke a sharp thorn from the bush he was under and carefully drained all the blisters on the bottoms of his feet and the backs of his legs. When the light began to fade he took off his shirt and wrapped half of it around each foot. Using a gnarled branch from a dead shrub he was able to manage a staggering walk.

He made his way to the first wash to the south, descended to its bottom, and slowly moved upstream. He checked the soft sand of its dry bed. Not far along he came across what he'd hoped to find: the faint markings of his tracks from four days earlier. He followed these up another slope.

The next canyon was deeper. He slid as quietly as he could to the bottom and paused. It was somewhere toward the head of this canyon that he had buried his supplies. The darkness was full now and Daniel took the time to readjust the clumsy wrappings on his feet. He sat on a large rock still hot from the sun and as he rested, his eyes played across the moonlit sand of the wash. His former prints showed as shallow scoops of darkness. But there was something else. The low angle of the light revealed a pattern of detail he might have missed in the brilliance of the day. There was a double impression—as if someone had stepped along in his prints.

Daniel continued to sit for a few moments, gathering his breath and strength. Then he reached for a sizable rock and began a slow, quiet walk up the canyon.

The shadows of the moonlight deepened as the walls of the canyon rose. He stayed as close to them as he could, avoiding the open sand. Ahead he began to see the rosy light of a fire. A faint odor of smoke. Carelessness? Or a trap?

Daniel stepped into the light of the fire. His glance took in the scattered contents of his knapsack. He continued to move. Always move in the face of danger. Force the issue.

He was still weak from sickness and dehydration, but his mind moved in familiar patterns. His eyes searched. He slipped forward more quickly, and a little to one side as the barest of sounds tinkled from behind and above. A large chunk of sandstone glanced from the back of his head. He sprawled forward in a relaxed, utterly limp fall. Another chunk of rock splattered just beyond him.

Blood flowed freely from under his hair. The blood mingled with fluid from his reopened sunburns and covered the exposed portions of his neck and face.

Brush stirred nearby and he listened to the ground as light steps approached. There was no sound to the steps, only a soft thumping that he *felt* with the skin of his cheek. At the last moment, he whirled, springing forward in a single fluid motion. A startled cry reached his ear as he whipped out with the gnarled stump end of his walking stick. It shattered against the forehead of the stooping figure. Daniel would have followed instantly with the rock he clutched in his other hand, but something crashed against the top of his skull and he sank forward in a sick lurch. Darkness engulfed him as he made feeble swimming motions with his hands.

Daniel stirred. Instinctively he tried to reject the world of fogged vision and pain that sprang into his mind. He searched for peace, darkness, and oblivion. They were not to be found. Nor were there individual points of pain. His whole body throbbed with a continuous ache.

Something moved in the foggy world around him and this shock brought his mind into focus. He shook his head with careful jerks. Nothing changed. The fog remained. It curled and swirled around him, rattling dry leaves and tugging at his hair. It was damp, gloriously wet. Just breathing it in was like drinking of the purest water.

The ocean, of course. There was bound to be fog from off the ocean. The fog was so thick he could see only a few feet. Water seemed to stick and drip from everything—shriveled bushes, rocks, even the buttons of his shirt.

Dimly he could see rations and other boxes scattered around. And the dead ashes of a fire. But it was movement that again caught his eye. A small animal was standing not four feet away, almost invisible in the fog. It was nibbling contentedly on the remains of a concentrated-ration pack.

It slowly penetrated Daniel's mind that some ridiculous-looking animal was eating *his* rations. Daniel lurched to his hands and knees. But the animal was instantly gone, springing away on tiny hoofed feet.

A goat? Daniel wondered about this as he stuffed bits of ration into his mouth. The taste of food cleared his head with a snap.

He glared around, searching for some kind of weapon. The contents of his knapsack were scattered everywhere. Boxes, half opened and discarded, littered the clearing. His need for a weapon dimmed. If his attacker still lived, then he, Daniel Trevor, would never have awakened. He set about collecting scattered equipment and repacking it carefully. He set up his still and began collecting the water he would shortly need.

The sun was already starting to burn through and break up the fog. He patched himself as well as he could and then went back and checked the scene of the previous night's battle. Here a rude shock awaited him. There was no body. The dry wood of his walking stick had shattered on impact. There was blood on the ground, but the body he'd struck had been able to drag itself away.

Daniel followed the signs on the ground. Not far away a bush rattled and he heard a groan. This reassured him. He would finish the job in short order.

He stumbled forward into one of the biggest bushes he'd yet seen on this island. It had thick, wax-covered branches and small leaves. Needlelike thorns pushed out in every direction to protect the leaves.

Daniel pushed at the bush with a stick, trying to see where his antagonist was hidden. Daniel could hear a soft moaning, but couldn't see through the thick foliage. He circled, but the bush was impenetrable. The moaning stopped. Daniel listened for a moment, then dropped to his hands and knees and began to crawl.

The branches were close to the ground, but aside from an outer shell of live growth the plant seemed dead. However, the waxy-green branches were still covered with thorns and he managed to find a few. Toward the center of the bush there was room enough to look around.

The girl was curled at the base of the bush. He noticed two things immediately: the soles of her feet, tough as leather; and the clot of blood and hair that covered the left side of her face. She was still alive and breathing strongly. This he regretted.

He watched for a moment. The tatters of clothing must be very old. Older than she was, he guessed. She must be in her middle teens. Probably a child from the last landing of colonists. Very thin. Probably underfed.

Daniel shook himself. There was no point in speculating and delaying what had to be done. He squirmed closer and it was then that he noticed her good eye was open and watching him.

"Don't come closer," she whispered. "I will kill you."

He paused. It was not what she said that bothered him, but the calmness in her voice. It took courage to speak calmly when you were about to die. Daniel felt a spark of admiration. Was there a valid reason for delaying her death? Perhaps he could make some use of her that would offset the danger she represented.

He began to back away. He would return to his camp for some water and there he could consider this problem in more leisure and be more objective.

"Don't leave." And now she was clearly begging—the strength of her will giving way a little to the weakness of her body. The breath rattled a little in her throat. She wanted so much to kill this man. But no one would find her here. She would die herself if she allowed him to leave.

Daniel Trevor stopped at the sound of her voice, and it wasn't by choice. Two branches of the bush had closed down behind him and were now blocking the way. He pushed at them impatiently and slowly became aware of their strange mobility. It was horrible to watch as the whole bush flowed in a slow fashion to block his progress.

"Help me," the girl whispered, barely audible. "Will you help me? You will live if you help me."

The bush paused in its motion and Daniel considered the implications of this. Very dangerous. Perhaps she could kill him. Or make the bush kill him. He watched her, thinking furiously. That sense of darkness came to him in smothering intensity for a moment and then lifted just as quickly.

The girl was twitching slightly now. The brightness faded from her eye. He could almost sense the struggle. Then slackness came into her face. At the same moment the plant rustled and began sagging back into its natural shape.

Daniel crawled quickly forward. He noted a faint pulse in her neck. Just for a second he hesitated. He would never have this full freedom of decision again.

Daniel cocked his head to one side in an attitude of listening. But in reality, his mind had gone blank. It was one of those rare moments in his life when there was some smell in the air—or some knot of darkness unraveling—that might be of the future. He tried to listen harder. The only thing that happened was a bristling of the hair at the back of his neck.

He shivered slightly and shook off the stillness. With the fingers of his right hand he turned the girl's face. He saw the bruised forehead and swollen eye. Dirty brown hair was matted with blood against her temple and left cheek. Her head rolled back when he released the chin.

Carefully, almost gently, he dragged her from under the bush and carried her back to his camp.

Chapter 4.

Derbid of the long sight was unhappy. The disappearance of his daughter was affecting him more than he cared to admit. She'd been gone six days now, ever since the day of the landing—when he'd sent her off to follow and do away with Daniel Trevor. When she hadn't returned that first night Derbid hadn't thought much of it. She wasn't a mindful child. She often went off to be alone—but never for this long. The need for food had always brought her back to the punishment she required.

She must be dead. It was the only explanation he could think of, and there was only one person who could have killed her. That was why he had demanded that Daniel Trevor be the first man the colonists surrender up. Derbid would get his revenge.

Grant, leader of the community, had smiled at Derbid's request, but Grant had agreed nonetheless. If this Trevor was a troublemaker, as Derbid insisted, then there was no reason not to make him the first. Grant wanted nothing to interfere with the Randolphs and the understanding that had been reached between them. And it was good to keep Derbid happy. Especially now that he was the community's sole contact with the Flame.

It was too bad about the girl. Derbid should have taken better care of her. Shouldn't have mistreated her so much. She'd been useful, but dangerous. You could hardly trust yourself to think when she'd been around. Most would be glad that she was gone, but not Grant. Do you put out your cooking fire just because it can burn you?

Grant shook his head. Such foolish thoughts people had. It was his responsibility as leader to see that foolish thoughts did not become foolish actions.

Grant returned his attention to the barren hillside. He was waiting now for the demanded man to be delivered. It was noon and nearly time for them to arrive. Grant stood alone in the open, but his men were nearby, hidden in the brush.

In the distance he could see three men toiling up the trail, two of them dragging the third. Grant recognized the two as Randolph brothers. The third must be the man named Daniel Trevor.

As they came closer, Grant frowned. The dragged man looked very old. It could not be the right man. Grant let his right hand drop to the knife at his side. The signal brought seven of his men out of hiding to surround the Randolph brothers.

George Randolph spoke rapidly. "I can explain! You can see that this isn't the man you asked for, but there's a reason. We brought him because he is the only one who can tell you where the man you want is.

"We did as you asked. We went to get the man you wanted, but he was gone. This old man was at his hut looting his supplies. We tried to get information from the old man, but he is unable to tell the truth. He tells a different story every time we ask. He even claims that one of us hired him to take the man you want into your land and dump him there." George shrugged nervously. "He's crazy."

Grant grunted at this. What was the truth? Had they killed Daniel Trevor for some reason of their own, or were they protecting him? No, there was no reason they would protect someone who threatened their leadership.

When Henry Randolph saw that the story Ralph had concocted was being accepted, and they were safe, he couldn't contain his curiosity any longer. "Do you really eat these guys?" he blurted out.

Grant frowned deeply, but before he could answer this insult Derbid stepped forward.

"Are you sure this Trevor is dead?" Derbid demanded. "I want to see his body before I will believe it!"

"I never said he was dead," George stammered. "I only said that we couldn't find him. He's not in the colony. We searched everywhere. Maybe the old man tossed his body into the ocean. How should I know?"

Derbid hissed. "Kill this one!" pointing at George. "He will talk straight before he dies!"

"SILENCE!" Grant ordered. "If you had taken better care of your daughter, we would know now if he spoke the truth!"

Derbid shrank back at the anger and truth in Grant's accusation.

"We will go now," Grant ordered. He motioned his men to pick up the limp and terrified old man. When they had moved away Grant turned to the waiting Randolphs. "If I find you have lied, you will not live a day beyond that."

Derbid hesitated, wanting to speak with these men further, but Grant glared at him. They moved off together and disappeared beyond the crest of a hill.

The Randolph brothers returned to the colony thankful to be alive.

Daniel watched her eat. She'd slept through the heat of the day and now all she wanted to do was eat. She ate more than he did.

You'd better be worth it, he thought. Her eyes fastened on him and they watched each other in a kind of distrustful silence.

She was a little better to look at now. He had cut away most of the hair and blood that had covered her face, leaving only the clot over the wound itself. This he had covered with a patch and tape. Her left eye was still bloodshot, but no longer blinded. A demon, he chuckled: one red eye, one white.

She glared at him, seeming to understand that she was the source of his humor. She reached for another ration pack.

"No," he said firmly, pushing the pack out of her reach with his walking stick. She blinked at him. Her feet were tied or she might have done something violent. It didn't occur to her that she should thank him for saving her life, giving her food. He was an enemy.

"Untie me!" she ordered.

He smiled sweetly but didn't move.

"Fool!" she screamed. "I'll kill you."

There was a trace of fear in her voice now and Daniel liked that a little better. She had guts though, or maybe was just stupid, trying to give him orders.

"Want some water?" he asked, taking a drink himself. She didn't answer, but her eyes watched as he changed the water bag on the still.

"How does it work?" she asked, when he was done.

"I'll show you," he answered, "the day you stop promising to kill me."

"I don't want to kill you now," she said, watching as the first drops of water dripped into the new bag.

Like fun, Daniel chuckled to himself. I like you better when you're honest about it.

She didn't like him laughing at her and she kicked her feet, testing the strength of the bond. "Free me," she said in frustration, "so I can cut your throat."

It was a challenge, Daniel realized. *She thinks I'm going to kill her and just wants a fair chance at me before she goes.*

"That's not the way to charm me into letting you go," he said, trying to sound reasonable. If she wasn't afraid maybe she would cooperate.

"What do you want?" she asked finally, sounding suddenly tired.

"Well, that's better. How about your name? What do your enemies call you?"

"Derl."

"And your friends?"

"I have no friends."

Daniel smiled. The girl didn't have much of a sense of humor, but that suited him just fine. "Well, Derl, I'll tell you what: If you agree to help me, I'll let you loose."

"Why would you want my help? What can I do that you cannot? Why do you play with me?" She turned her head away and closed her eyes.

Damn it, he thought, suddenly angry. *Stupid. She is stupid.* He got up, moved toward her, and reached for her arm.

"Stay away," she cried. She kicked his leg with both her feet and he fell.

He grabbed her arm, twisted it behind her, sat on her legs, and began to tie her wrists together behind her back. She struggled wildly. He could feel her legs grinding against the rocks in her efforts to twist free.

"Stop it!" he shouted, shaking her violently, turning her head so she had to look at him. "I'm not going to kill you. Understand! Get that through your head?"

He pushed her away, feeling tired. He wanted to sleep, but he couldn't—not while her hands were free. So he tied her.

He moved to a safe distance. She had turned away from him, curled up, and now she was shaking violently. Whether it was from fear, relief, or anger, he didn't care. He dropped to the ground and fell asleep almost instantly.

The girl did not sleep immediately. Never in her life had she wanted to kill as much as she did at that moment. Never had she been so helpless to carry out her wish. He frightened her. Her father had hurt her, many times, but she had never been frightened like this. She'd never met anyone whom she couldn't touch, who wasn't there.

She reflected on these things and looked in Daniel's direction. What could she do? How could she free herself and still satisfy her curiosity about this man, his strange mind, and the machine that made water? She wanted to know about these things.

She fell asleep and dreamed that she had killed him, but was still able to talk to him and learn about what he was.

They were both asleep when the goat first returned. It descended into the canyon, ledge by ledge, on quietly clicking hoofs. It moved toward them hesitantly, its nature struggling against the will that forced it on. Its eyes were lighted with an intelligence that did not belong to it, an intelligence that did not belong on Earth.

It stopped by the girl. Swiftly it began to nibble on the bonds that held her. She woke, frightened, but when she saw what it was, she smiled. The goat was her guardian, the shadowing presence she had known all her life. Even her father would not harm her when the goat was near.

She watched, fascinated, as it chewed, its eyes burning into her. In flashes she could sense and see the face of something within or beyond the goat. And it looked back at her.

This was something new and frightening. She had never seen it so clearly before. She shivered uncontrollably.

Daniel moved and the goat was suddenly still. Its eyes were no longer on the girl. It stood, head cocked, hesitating; then it was gone as swiftly as it had come.

"What was that?" Daniel's eyes were open. He was looking around in the midnight darkness.

"Nothing," the girl said with surging confidence. "It was nothing, just like you are nothing."

"What's that supposed to mean?"

She smiled. "I will help you now."

Daniel sat up, frowning. His head still ached from the pounding she'd given it with sandstone. Now she wanted to help. He crawled to her, turned her over roughly, and examined the rope around her arms and legs. Then he turned her back and began examining her swollen eye. "Hold still," he said gently as she jerked back away from the pain. "Do you know of a place to hide where neither your people nor mine could find us?" he asked, releasing her.

She pushed back a short distance from him, sitting awkwardly in her bonds. "Yes," she nodded.

"Can we reach it in what's left of the night?"

Again she nodded.

Daniel gathered up as much of the supplies as he could comfortably carry. The rest he buried as well as he could. He removed the rope from the girl's legs and slipped it around her still-bound wrists. She watched in silence as he tested what was to be her lead rope. He shrugged his pack on with a groan. "Let's go," he ordered.

Derl smiled oddly as she rose to her feet. She led him down the canyon to the beach and into ankle-deep water. "No tracks," she murmured. She continued to smile, kicking at the water as she walked, turning back occasionally—walking backward, pulling with a laugh at the rope.

"You don't have to walk so far ahead," Daniel said.

She dropped back immediately and walked meekly at his side.

"What are they like?" he asked. "Your people."

She spoke slowly at first, then in a rush: There were seventy-two adults and fifty-six children. They all lived near the south of the island, mostly in a large and very deep canyon. This canyon had the island's only freshwater springs, but she could find water elsewhere—in springs and seeps—for weeks and weeks after a good rain. Mostly she ate goats, sometimes chickens and quail. There were fish and gooey shellfish from the beaches. Small patches of corn, beans, and tomatoes grew near the springs in the wet canyon.

Daniel listened until she wound down into silence. "Where did goats, chickens, and quail come from?" he asked. "They didn't come down on any of the ships. Are they native to this island?"

Derl hesitated. For a moment her secret hatred of this man almost swelled to the surface. Then she calmed herself. "They come from the Flame," she said slowly, "as reward for our work."

"What is *the Flame,* as you say it?" he asked. "Is that where you cook your food?"

Derl laughed, then quickly fell into silence. "I'll show you," she promised, looking directly into his eyes. "Someday you will see the Flame for yourself."

Daniel began to feel that the Flame was something he'd rather not see. Maybe that was where they roasted colonists.

The beach began to break up into rocky ground and they were quiet as they scrambled through the rocks together. Finally the beach ended altogether and a cliff rose to block their path. "How much farther?" Daniel asked, staring ahead into the darkness and sound of breakers crashing against the cliff.

"Not far. We must climb here." She paused. "I cannot go with my hands tied."

"O.K.," he agreed.

They climbed together. She helped pull him over a lip of the cliff. Then for twenty minutes they crossed a plain of withered brush. At last came a drop of twenty feet into an obscure and sheltered gully. Here, under an overhanging rock, Derl sank to her knees and smoothed the sand.

"This is the place," she said.

Daniel looked around. He took a deep breath. There were no odors of fire, cooking, or previous occupation. It was possibly a good spot.

"We can sleep here," Daniel agreed. He drew the coiled rope from his belt.

She stared at him. Then her lips twisted slightly and she came closer and allowed her hands and legs to be bound and drawn together behind her back. She could not sleep comfortably and so she laid awake and waited for her goat to come.

Derl stood in the darkness, her hands and legs gloriously free. She looked at the sleeping man. She could kill him, but that would not be enough. No one had done what he had done. No one had made her afraid without touching, without hurting her. But he had.

Death was too easy. And there was her promise. She had promised to show him the Flame. Alive he would see it. Alive and a prisoner he would know what it was to be in terror of something *he* did not understand. Just as she had been. Just as she had not understood him.

Yes, he would be a prisoner. He would be bound and helpless before *her*.

Daniel woke with a start. Something was wrong. He smelled smoke; black sticky sooty smoke. The girl was gone and so was his knapsack. He cursed and started to follow her tracks. But what he saw above stopped him. A thick column of black smoke rose from the top edge of the gully. He scrambled up the slope.

The fire was just going out when he reached it, but the damage was already done. Far off in the distance he could see a small group of people moving across the level ground. They were coming in his direction. He had perhaps twenty minutes before they could reach him.

Scrambling back down to the campsite he found that Derl hadn't taken everything. Much of his heavy equipment, including the case with his rifle and ammunition, had been dumped behind a bush. She had taken all of his food and the water still, but nothing of which she did not know the use.

He considered his possible courses of action. He could run, but even without the rifle he could never outdistance them. He could try hiding, but rejected this as impossible on ground they were familiar with. That left only one choice: fight.

He picked the spot carefully: a little mound on the edge of the plain. His back was to the sea, a long way down, and his right was covered by a sharp drop into the gully, about twenty yards away. The mound gave him a good view of the flat ground in front of him and to his left. He could keep them from reaching the gully and be assured of two safe directions.

When he had settled in place, he took time to look through the remainder of his pack. Along with the rifle and ammunition there were half a dozen power cells and several empty plastic water bags. That little idiot, he thought to himself. Without power cells the water still would do her just the amount of good she deserved.

He wrapped the cells in an empty plastic bag and buried them carefully. Into another bag he jammed all of his ammunition except for three twelve-shot clips. These he would need for immediate use.

They were getting closer now and he hurriedly assembled the rifle. The smoke from the signal fire Derl had set was now gone and the sky was a sharp clear blue against the brown land. Daniel rested in the shade of a rock and waited. It wouldn't be long. He could hear their voices. Six men were in front and several others were lagging well behind, out of range. All of them were heavily bearded and dirty. Their faces held the eager hungry look of successful hunters.

Daniel sank closer to the earth. He powdered his face with dust. The first move would be theirs.

Chapter 5.

The early-morning sun had revealed the smoke to Grant, first as a wisp of gray and then as a thick black column.

Grant was in no hurry. It was not the leader's job to hurry. He let the younger generation dash ahead and take the risks but he kept his sons with him. They were restless but he considered it part of his job to see that they came of age knowing what leadership meant. He was giving them a lecture on the present situation.

"If either of you expect to become leader some day, you will have to learn to listen to me. You must think before you act. Leave the acting to others. It is not the leader's job to act."

Joe, his eldest son, was impatient. "If we do not hurry Ferd and Joel will be the first to the fire. They will get the glory of the capture."

"What makes you think there will be anyone to capture?" Grant asked reasonably.

"But surely only a new colonist would make a smoky fire like that."

"Possibly. But whoever made the fire also traveled many miles through our land without being seen. Even if there is a capture to be made Joel and Ferd may find it more difficult than they expect." He pointed at the knee-high brush covering the ground. "Just because new colonists are new here does not mean they have no brains. Anyone could be hiding in this brush and those two in front would run past without knowing. No," he said sadly, "Ferd and Joel will not live long enough to become leader. They will be sought after by women but other men will never let them be leader. They will be hated by those who are not heroes. No, a leader must be thoughtful and careful. He cannot afford to take unnecessary chances with the lives of those he leads, nor can he offend others with his pride."

Neither of his sons were listening. They were watching the two figures far ahead of everyone else now. Joel and Ferd had come up to the dying fire and stopped. They were pointing and shouting. They had seen the hunted; he was backed into a corner with nowhere to go. They started toward the knoll where the man was trying to hide himself.

Grant's sons could wait no longer. They ran forward. They could not get there first but perhaps they could help. Grant shook his head. His sons were still young. With time they might learn.

The waiting was over. Daniel watched as the two racing toward him drew their knives. A coldness came into his heart. He tasted a dark bitterness as time and space seemed to press in on him. His teeth came together in anger and something like a spasm snapped through his body. He felt an odd lurch of detachment. He no longer looked out from behind his eyes. Mind and body became tools to be used, ruthlessly. Pain no longer distracted.

The rifle sight rested on the closer of the two. The trigger squeezed slowly. There was mild surprise when it went off. The leading figure twirled in midstride and crashed into the brush, rolling and sliding into the gully.

The bolt was sliding closed and the trigger squeezed again. The second figure flipped in the air once, landing on its back. The bolt was sliding and the trigger squeezing, but the third shot was never fired.

Daniel took a deep, ragged breath—his first since snapping his teeth together. The targets were gone. He would not waste shots on speculation. He wiped at his face absently. A sheen of sweat had sprung out there without him noticing.

Derl struggled with her awkward burden. Her goal was a high bluff where she could overlook the capture. But she moved slowly. She did not feel the victory and triumph that were rightfully hers. Instead she was tired and felt a dull apprehension at what her father would do when he discovered she was alive.

She did not hear the shots that killed Joel and Ferd, but when she reached her vantage point she could see their bodies. She could also see Daniel resting behind a mound of dirt and waiting. Only after listening to the thoughts of Grant and his sons did she learn how the two men had died. And she had caused it. Her fire had brought two members of the community to their deaths.

How could a water still and the bits of food she had stolen make up for this? She waited for fear for herself to engulf her at these thoughts, but nothing happened. She did not care.

Her mind seemed clouded with odd thoughts and feelings. She wanted to be sick. She wanted the Flame to take her away from this island where she would always be alone and would never care.

Perhaps they will kill him, she thought, but didn't want it. She wanted to keep her promise. She would send him through the Flame. Maybe then she would have the strength to follow.

The heat of the day passed slowly. Daniel was careful to keep his mind off gloomy thoughts about his impending demise. You did not survive by worrying. You did it by thinking. He kept his mind clear by working on two problems: the heat and escape.

He worked on heat first, because without water he had to stay cool. The shade of his rock pile disappeared as the morning sun climbed toward noon. The ground became broiler hot and he almost wished for the huge granite boulders that he and his father had hated so intensely. Those boulders had made his father's land on Trent worthless for farming, but they had provided cool shade all day long.

At the moment, though, he had only crumbling sandstone to work with and there was no way to make shade from it. He looked at the few withered plants on the knoll with him. They were fighting a losing battle with the sun as it was. Pitiful things. They couldn't even shade themselves, let alone a man.

The closest healthy-looking brush was a good fifty yards away in the wrong direction. This objection was overcome by the increasing heat. He walked down the gentle slope of his hill, placed his rifle in a handy spot, and started pulling and breaking. He was wrestling with the trunk of his second bush when he caught a blur of motion in the corner of his eye.

A hundred yards away two men were standing and whirling something over their heads. He watched for a second, puzzled, then jumped for his rifle. The movement saved him. The first pebble hummed by his ear. The second landed just short, splattered gravel, and careened into his thigh. The two men were gone before he could get off a shot.

Quickly Daniel limped back up the hill, dragging his brush with him. All in all, the risk had been worth taking. The brush would give him shade, and the bruise would give him respect. Both would prolong his life a bit.

With the heat problem solved, he began to concentrate on escape. He started by examining the landscape above and beyond the plain over which he fought. To his right, south, the island rose higher in one continuous sweep. It was cut by increasingly deeper canyons. Good country for a goat, but not for him in his present condition. Even supposing he slipped in that direction during the dark, he would never last through all the climbing. To his left, north and back toward the colony, the ground sank into gentler configuration. But this was where most of the savages concentrated. He could see them moving occasionally and more were slipping onto a ridge directly at his front. They wanted to force him south, deeper into their own broken land. He would not oblige. In any direction he ran, they would be faster and stronger. Well, he stopped at that thought. There was one way they would be even.

He left his knoll and crawled to the edge of the cliff. He threw a rock out and away, counting. One, two, three, four seconds, and he saw the splash. Three hundred feet! More than four seconds to fall all that way. He shivered and crawled back to his knoll.

Nothing had changed; they weren't going to move until it was dark. He began to think. Was it possible to climb down? Could *he* do it? Think he ordered himself: Think of a way.

The time passed by inches and he began to think of a way. He crawled back to the cliff edge and looked down. The day was starting to turn cold, a wind was blowing from the south. Big clouds were building in the distance.

When he got down, what then? No beach, but there was a line of rocks offshore and big breakers were beginning to show that the water close to the shore was shallow. Everything between the offshore rocks and the cliff was a cauldron of smooth rocks and potholes. You could maybe walk down there or be chewed to pieces depending on your luck and the tide.

He was going to try.

Once he decided, Daniel began working rapidly. He dumped his supplies again, this time with something in mind. There was a small shovel with a folding handle, which he had ignored as useless before. Now it was precious. He fitted his foot in the face of the shovel and began wrapping with cloth and surgical tape. The folding handle braced against his ankle and calf. The lip of the shovel overlapped his toes by several inches. His toes were too weak to cling to tiny crevices, but with the shovel he might do it. The cliff face was soft—

sandstone and junk. Handholds and whole slabs of it might flake away, but with his shovel foot he might be able to reach solid stuff. The remaining cloth and tape he wrapped around his right hand. It would be a glove on his holding arm and he would use his knife and the front section of his rifle barrel as pitons, slipping them into any cracks and fractures he could use.

He took a last look from his knoll, then disassembled the rest of his rifle and put it in the pack along with ammunition and several inflated water bags. The rest of these bags he inflated like balloons, tied off, and fastened to his belt.

Quickly he searched the cliff edge, looking for a way down that didn't involve overhangs. He chose a shallow trough where a tiny watershed plunged over the cliff. Laying flat on his stomach, he began to back toward the edge. He held the knife in his right hand and had the short section of rifle barrel jammed into his pants. He pushed his shovel foot out into empty air and soon both his legs up to his thighs were over the edge and without support. He began to slip. He dug the knife into the soft dirt, but it didn't do anything but slow him down. Frantically he scratched with his left hand. He had to slow down.

His waist went over and he could reach his feet down, but he was sliding too fast. The shovel and his toes scraped without catching. As his chest began to slide over the edge, he grabbed at a root with his left hand and it held.

He panted, shaking. Don't get scared, he told himself. Don't do that or your muscles will turn to jelly. He hung on to the root and rested, trying to get used to the idea. No turning back now.

He looked down carefully. The cliff wasn't vertical. Just very steep. He felt with his toes and shovel, knocking away dirt and digging a small ledge. He dug another for his left foot and tested them both. They held. With his knife he began to dig several handholds. When these were done he let go of the root. Everything held and he felt confidence returning.

Slowly and carefully he began to fall into a routine: Lower right leg, dig footholds, secure, lower left leg to level with right, dig handholds with knife, first right, then left, secure, lower right leg again. It went on and on. The edge of the cliff receded. His whole body began to learn how to hold on. His ears, chin, elbows, stomach, knees. Everything was touching something and he always moved slowly. Never gain momentum. Never stress the crumbling stuff to the breaking point once you are resting on it.

He was down fifty feet when he noticed a change. The softness had gone out of the rock. His shovel wouldn't dig anymore. He looked down. A harder sandstone was below him. There was no give in it, but there were cracks between layers and vertical fractures. He reached down with his soft foot and found that it would be better to lead with this now and feel with his toes for the cracks and ledges.

It was almost like a ladder now, it was easy. He climbed down rapidly making another hundred feet before his luck ran out.

The top of the cliff was out of sight now because the layered sandstone was steeper than the soft stuff above it. This hard stuff now ended and he was faced with a brittle and crumbly shale that was no good for anything. There was a gap of about ten feet and below that more hard sandstone. He shifted sideways. There was a crack in the face of the cliff. It must have been a small fault, because the crumbly shale layer was shifted down almost twenty feet, all at once.

Daniel worked down on the new side of the crack and was able to get below and cross under the shale layer.

He began to move down quickly again, on a new stairway of sandstone. The sound of the breakers was coming closer and getting louder in his ears.

Just fifty feet to go and then it happened. He put his foot into a crack on top of a wide and inviting layer of solid sandstone. It held beautifully for a second and he was lowering his shovel foot toward the next layer when it just disappeared. It was as quiet and smooth as an elevator.

He grabbed with his hands, and his feet scrambled against nothing but air and dust. Below him there was a crash like the end of the world and everything shuddered. Dust rose from the face of the cliff as if it had been a dirty curtain whacked with a stick. Pebbles and gravel rained down from above.

Daniel closed his eyes and pulled himself and his feet back to solid ground. He looked below him. There was nothing there. Fifty feet of air and a broken jumble of fresh rock washing in the surf.

The overhang was everywhere, extending on both sides of him as far as he could see. Then he remembered the fault. Moving sideways, he found it again. He gained another fifteen feet this way, but the same overhang was below him again. Thirty-five feet to the water.

Hanging by his hands he could reduce that to less than thirty, but it was still too far.

Clouds were everywhere now and it was getting darker. The wind had shifted and was coming from the west now. There was the smell of rain in every gust. He had to get down now, while there was light and the rocks were dry.

He moved to the edge of the fault again, staying on the solid rock on his side of it, but examining the soft stuff that had fallen away to cause the overhang. He could get at it here, at the edge of the fault, but would it hold?

He took the short section of rifle barrel from his belt and reached as far toward the soft stuff as he could. He poked at it with the steel and it crumbled away. No good.

It was starting to rain. Daniel hurried. He jammed the rifle barrel as far as he could into the last crack in solid rock, as close as he could get it to the wall of soft rock. Gripping it with both hands, he swung out and both his feet touched the soft rock, but there was nothing they could get a hold on. He had expected this, but he needed to get as close to it as he could. There was just enough slope in it that if he got flat against it and slid, it would slow him down.

He let go of the rifle barrel and dropped. His feet, legs, arms, and everything else he had, touched as much of the face of rock as they could. He was sliding faster, his shirt and pants shredding. Faster. His skin began to burn. He pushed away with all his strength and he was dropping free. He kicked at a jutting rock that tried to reach out at him, and then he was in the water, sinking. The air bags in his pack and on the back of his belt spun him around and jerked him to a sudden halt.

He struggled not to open his mouth. He kicked and searched with his feet. Finally he was standing on slippery rock and breathing as fast as he could. A wave washed over him and he staggered, gagging water. He felt weak everywhere. But he was down. He couldn't stop now.

He struggled seaward. There were rocks and potholes everywhere. He slipped and fell, cursing the shovel. It was like an ice skate on these slimy rocks. He continued to move outward and it got easier. He could see huge swells moving in and smashing themselves against a wall of rocks. It was the highest of those rocks he was trying to reach.

Clouds of spray, whipped by the wind, ebbed and flowed around him. Half the sky was covered by an impenetrable wall of clouds. Looking back, he could see movement on the cliff above. There was a splash, and a flung rock skimmed by. Daniel moved faster, ignoring the shouts and protesting voices that reached after him.

Occasional waves washed over the barrier and knocked him off his feet, but he was getting closer, and the splashes of thrown rocks were getting farther behind.

The sun was gone and he tried to find the rock outcrop he was searching for, but the sea and sky were both black. The force of the wind was increasing and more and more waves washed over the seawall. A giant swell loomed out of the darkness and gently lifted him off his feet. He treaded water. The swell passed and he was still treading water.

He was in deep water and there was nothing to do but float and pray the waves didn't bash him to pieces against the very rocks he had been trying to reach.

The storm continued to build. It lashed against the island in a frenzy at being blocked. The wind gusted and swells got bigger and more turbulent. Flashes of lightning began to reveal cliffs and beaches, and Daniel realized that he was moving fast in a line parallel to the island. What would happen when it was gone?

He put this thought away and concentrated on breathing. Suddenly he felt his feet entangled and he was surrounded by a gray mass of floating seaweed. It dragged at him and he kicked frantically, suddenly grateful again for the shovel that was cutting him free.

The mass of weeds pulled him into an eddy and suddenly there was a mass of blackness looming up ahead. The whole mass of weed lurched and flung itself at shore. He covered his head with his arms and then there was nothing but darkness and pain.

Chapter 6.

Rain poured in a steady stream. Grant sat huddled in the goatherd's hut. It had taken Grant six hours to climb to the top of the island and reach this point, but he was too late. The mud and darkness had delayed him and now he could no longer enter the wet canyon. Its dry streambeds were now a churning mass of boulders and mud, rushing downward. He could only hope that all his people had reached the safety of the cliffhouses. The little patches of corn and vegetables would be gone, and perhaps many goats would be caught in the deep canyons. He had never seen so much rain.

Derbid had come with Grant, arguing and shouting all through the six hours of their difficult climb on the muddy slopes of the island. Grant was now too tired and angry to continue with it.

"No!" Grant said at last, emphatically, to end all argument. "The matter is finished."

"I will leave now," Derbid countered. He was determined to find Daniel Trevor's body and make sure it was dead.

"You do and you will leave the long sight behind. You will not bother to come back."

Derbid couldn't believe his ears. Grant dared to threaten him!

"Don't be mistaken, Derbid. I mean what I say. I am speaking as leader of the community. Important things must be done first. Your eyes are no good to us when they refuse to see. What good is his body? If he is alive, could you kill him alone? No. So do as you are supposed to do. Report this at once. Only you can speak directly to the Flame."

Derbid was livid with anger. "I determine what the Flame wills. My daughter, the daughter of the Flame, is dead at the hands of this man. It will want proof of his death."

"*If* it demands, then we will search. I will not risk your life without that demand."

"You will not remain leader long," Derbid threatened. "When the

Flame learns you have hindered its will, you will be swept from the face of the Earth."

Grant rose in anger. "Do as I command. We will go to the Flame now and hear what it wishes in this matter. Forget your daughter. Others have lost as much today and they are working instead of crying their grief in public."

Derbid shrank back at this accusation. But he could not forget his daughter because she was still alive. He had seen her tracks while others had been trying to capture Daniel Trevor. The rain had hidden them from others, but for how long? If they found she had been the cause of two deaths things would not go well for her. He had to find her himself and warn her of what to say. And he must also make sure Daniel Trevor was dead and could not say how it had really happened. Nothing else was safe. Nothing else would work.

For a long time Derl was content to watch. Her father's people didn't waste effort and she knew that the search they were making was not for her. She was both interested and amazed by their movements along the beaches and cliffs. It could only mean that Daniel Trevor was still alive.

Deep in the pit of her stomach Derl felt a growing fear. Never had she felt this way before. Even her father's beatings were nothing to make her fear. She could understand them. But this man was different. He had resisted her power. He had survived her betrayal. Now he was alive and she could almost feel his wrath seeking her.

She continued to watch the search closely. All day they hunted at the water's edge and found nothing. It was the way they searched that chilled her. They went in groups of three and looked with such reluctance she suspected they didn't want to find him.

Derl hugged her sides in silent misery. She had black thoughts of her own future and cried for herself.

The mood passed and Derl lay exhausted. She watched a few clouds scuttle across the sky, stragglers from the previous day. The air was clear and the infinite expanse of water a deep blue. On such days she would sometimes climb high to the top of the island and look to the east from the edge of the great and most tremendous of cliffs. From there, across miles and miles of water, she could see great expanses of a land she could never reach. It was a dream of hers that somehow, someday, she would cross those waters and reach a land where desert ended and something else grew. But today she didn't dream her dream. Instead she watched the terrible yellow sun slowly grow softer and glow a red orange as it sank to the sea.

For a fleeting moment the soft light transformed the harsh desert landscape into something of beauty. But the moment passed and the sun slid into the water. The glow faded and stark reality returned. She wondered at the feeling this sight always produced in her and somehow she didn't regret that it was gone. Such things were meant to be brief.

Darkness brought a growing sense of purpose to her. Never in her life had she been more comfortably situated. She could live without effort for ten whole days. Food, water, shelter, and freedom; she had them all and yet was miserable. Therefore she must act to remove her misery.

She would do what the others were afraid to do. She would find the man. She would make him like her. He had power. She had power. Together they could rule the community. They could rule the whole island.

She knew she could find him, because like all people, she could sense his presence. When she got close enough, within a mile or two, she could feel him and know that he was alive. Once she had sensed this, she could also tell in which direction he lay. It was only then that he became different and she could see the dark and shining reflections. She could not listen, but she could find him.

There was danger in this. He could kill her. Perhaps he would. But he hadn't done it before. Wasn't it better to try this than to be miserable and hated all her life?

She felt a new strength come to her with this determination. She would do something of her own choosing. She would become a person of her own will.

Derbid had given up his arguments. The walk to the end of the island was ten miles from the goatherd's hut. Even under the clouds of the retreating storm the trail was hot, already drying, and without shade. It snaked its way along the barren backbone of the island and at time came to the very edge of the great cliff itself. Just looking down made Derbid queasy. The great cliff towered more than fifteen hundred feet high in many places. Crashing waves at the base thundered. The sound was so close it roared, but the waves were so distant they seemed a fine and changing pattern of spider web.

As the day advanced the trail descended toward the southern tip of the island and they approached the end of their journey. Derbid could make out the bony finger of land where the Flame burned. It was surrounded on three sides by cliffs, and the neck connecting it to the cliff trail was guarded day and night.

The Flame itself was just a small fire kept continually burning in a thick grid of steel. It wasn't visible during the day, burning as it did against a background of red-brown sandstone. Only the heat shimmer of transparent smoke could be seen if looked for closely.

The sun was setting when Derbid's tired group crossed the low neck and mounted the rock tower where the Flame lay. They were challenged by the Flame's keeper. Derbid gave the ritual answer and they climbed the last fifty feet to the top. The rocky tower was barren of brush and shelter except for a pile of fuel for the Flame and a small hut to shelter the keeper. Derbid and the men with him sat and rested for a moment.

Derbid chewed a leathery chunk of meat and steeled himself for the meeting he must have with the Flame. He glanced at the steel grid with the Flame inside and then at the empty grid next to it. The empty grid was where he would contact the spirit of the Flame. But first he must gain its attention.

He picked up a rock and carefully tossed it into the center of the empty ring. At first, nothing happened, then very slowly the rock faded and was gone.

Settling back, Derbid began his wait. He would wait until the Flame saw fit to answer his call, and this was not always promptly. As was normal on such occasions, more wood was added to the fire. The Flame grew higher and hotter. No demons could come through it and reach the community. But their messenger could.

A shining metal sphere appeared suspended in the air above the Flame. It was the demon's messenger and it spoke.

"What is your message?"

Derbid turned to two of Grant's men and pointed at the captive they had brought along. The old man struggled and cried out but the two bearded guards ignored his efforts and lifted him. They bound him hand and foot, then threw him into the empty ring. Derbid watched impassively as the old man continued to struggle weakly. Finally the old man faded and disappeared, consumed by the spirit of the Flame. A full minute passed before the metal sphere spoke again.

"The message was garbled. Messenger nonfunctional. Report by direct contact."

Derbid swallowed. He'd been afraid this would happen. He had told the old man everything the demons needed to know, but, being eaten, the old man must have gone crazy or died. Derbid would never be sure which because no one ever returned from the Flame. Only goats and other food came through it when the demons were pleased with the prisoners the community supplied them.

Derbid prepared himself slowly. What would happen when they read the bad news in his mind? Could he hide anything from them? He tried to keep thoughts of Derl from his mind as he lowered himself into position. Surely they would be angry with her. He made his mind as blank as he could. He placed his head between two bars of the empty grid and waited.

The men around him watched anxiously. They saw his head slowly fade and waver.

He could feel it happening. The Flame was inside his head now with many voices. Derbid listened to their conversation but he couldn't take part because it was in a language of pictures and feelings that he could only partially translate. One of the voices was speaking what it read from his mind and another asked questions.

"What was new weapon?"

"A simple chemical projectile type."

"Any special function?"

"None observed."

"Did owner of weapon survive?"

"Unknown, but possible."

"Is experimental breeding subject to be returned on schedule?"

"No. Missing. She is missing. Native agent is interfering with subject and schedule."

Derbid knew they were speaking of his daughter and he tried harder to resist the pulling on his brain.

"Have him bring her here," the voice continued. "Also bring weapon and owner if possible. They are to be delivered to us. Administer punishment."

A pain clamped down on Derbid's head and he screamed. He resisted the commands he was given for only a moment. When his will yielded the pain eased and the punishment ended. He would do what was asked.

For a moment the men watching were afraid that Derbid's head would vanish from the ring completely, and the shout of pain came from a weak and pale shadowhead. If it had gone completely, eaten like the old man, then it would have meant his death.

Derbid staggered to his feet. His mind was a whirl of frightening orders. His daughter, the child of his only wife, was to be given to the Flame—to the demons that the Flame held back. He wept. His wife had come from the Flame and returned to it. Now they wanted his daughter to return as well.

A goat skittered up the rocks of the Flame's tower and stood before Derbid. Its eyes blazed with an eager redness.

Derbid covered his face. This was the goat that would betray his daughter. It would lead them to her and she would be taken.

Daniel crawled to the summit of the small islet where the storm had deposited him. He drank rainwater caught in the hollows of rocks.

Only three hundred yards separated his islet from the main island. He watched all through the day as searchers combed the beaches of the main island, but they never ventured to cross the short strip of water and check his islet. This he found strange, but more dangerous were the watchers posted on the cliffs and high hills overlooking the beach. Because of these he was forced to cower behind a clump of broken rocks throughout the whole day.

He kept his rifle ready, but this was not of much use. He was so exhausted that he slept much of the time and they could have collected him easily if they'd had the courage to swim the distance.

His islet was one of a string of rocks forming a point on the main island. As he examined his situation, Daniel began to understand how close he had come to being swept into the open ocean. The seaweed in which he had become trapped had probably saved his life.

The night passed in a cold and restless sleep. Hunger had reduced him to looking at bugs and beach creatures with appetite. Another day would kill him. The rainwater was gone and he was almost too weak to move. If he waited he could never swim the three hundred yards to the main island.

He prepared to leave at the first light of day. If there were no watchers he would kill a goat and survive a little longer. He would take nothing but his rifle and one extra clip of ammunition. The rest he would leave. It would be safer on this islet anyway.

He slipped down among the rocks and crept toward the water. Fog covered the land. Only the beaches and water were clear of it. Everything else was lost in its fuzzy white ceiling. He could almost reach up and put his hand into it.

As he crept closer to the beach, he froze. There was movement on the beach of the main island.

Daniel slid the rifle to his shoulder. The rifle was shorter, its front section and sight having been lost in cliff climbing, but he could still hit at this distance. The fog would muffle the sound and obscure the direction. He had to get across and he couldn't wait.

It was the girl. Daniel recognized the ragged pants and thin, tails-flapping shirt. She was walking fast and he would wait until she stopped. She ran a little, then walked again.

It was almost by instinct that she stopped and looked across at him, like an animal would. She couldn't see him, but she could see the island. He tightened the trigger, but his arm shook. It wasn't a sure shot. He waited, letting the trigger slacken. Maybe she would go away.

But she didn't. Instead she waded into the water and began to swim toward him. The water was smooth as glass and he watched as her awkward strokes brought her closer. He relaxed. She could not escape now and he would wait.

She struggled ashore, water streaming from her hair and clothes. Daniel was arrested by the form of her body beneath the wet clothing. He knew with a kind of certainty that this was his last chance to kill her, unaware, without having to meet her eye as he did it. But he couldn't. There was something in him that wouldn't let him. Maybe the knowledge that she was something unfinished, unformed. Something potential.

He tried to smile cynically, to think of some reason to let her live, to overlook the danger and betrayal behind her bright eyes. The reasons were there. But they faded before his enjoyment of just watching her move.

He tried to shake himself loose. It must be hunger, exhaustion, the nearness of his own death. What was he thinking of? She wouldn't hesitate to kill him. She had tried her best.

She was coming closer and she stopped suddenly as she saw him move, leveling his rifle. She also saw the awful coldness and resolution in his face.

"Don't kill me now!" she cried. She sank to the ground in a fit of tears and rage. "Not now!" She almost burst with anger and frustration.

Daniel could only pause and watch. There was no fear in her. He'd never seen so much violence in an unmoving form. She was shaking, almost as if she would burst from her body and strangle him for his stupidity in thwarting her plans.

This was better. This he could deal with. He laid aside his rifle with a shaken relief that he was no longer confronted with a girl of beauty and potential.

She noticed the change immediately, sprang up eagerly, and ran toward him. "I brought food," she said, producing part of a ration pack.

He grabbed it and swallowed it down in two choking bites.

"Hurry," she urged. "We have to swim back before the fog is gone."

Daniel found himself being pulled toward the water. He was too weak to resist, and actually enjoyed leaning against her. This was bad, he realized. If he was too weak to walk, how could he swim three hundred yards of water?

But this was solved for him. She pushed him in and he was forced to shove the rifle through his belt and swim for it. She splashed near him with inexpert energy and he concentrated on smooth, energy-saving strokes. It seemed to go on forever. He switched to a backstroke to make breathing easier. He wished he hadn't eaten so quickly. He could feel his stomach knotting. He wanted to drop the rifle but couldn't stop for fear of sinking. Suddenly he was in gentle breakers and could feel sand beneath his feet.

She was next to him immediately, guiding him along the beach and toward a bluff that was becoming clearer in the thinning fog.

"Hurry," she urged, pushing and pulling with impatient force.

They were among some rocks when he gasped and collapsed. His arms and legs felt like jelly. She dragged and he crawled. Then he fell and wouldn't move anymore.

It was full daylight when Daniel opened his eyes again. "Where are we?" he asked vaguely.

When no one answered, Daniel shook himself awake and sat up. He was lying in a hollow of rocks. The islet where he'd washed ashore was clearly visible across the water. There was food and a bag containing water next to him.

He ate and drank slowly. He was on the backside of a high knoll of land hidden from the main portion of the island. Crawling toward the top of this he was stopped by a shining object among the rocks. It was a piece of broken glass. It was the first glass he'd seen on the island. Nothing landed from the ship had been made of old-fashioned breakable glass.

As he climbed he found more of this and became puzzled. At the top of the knoll he found the source: a thick concrete pedestal. On top of the concrete was a rusted metal framework. Glass was still clinging to the outer edge of this framework. Daniel crept closer, keeping the cementwork between him and the overlooking hills. There was a mounting inside the metal framework that had probably revolved at one time. As he looked at this Daniel finally realized what the structure was. It was a lighthouse.

It overlooked the water in three directions and must have been automated. He touched it now with a kind of awe. This was something of the old Earth, before the decline. He wondered how long the light had burned after it had been forgotten, when there were no more ships to guide.

Perhaps a long time. The glass had probably been broken by some of the early Beta Colony settlers, the ancestors of the girl he was looking for.

A pebble struck him in the back and he whirled. The girl was below him, gesturing angrily. He climbed down to her and followed her back to the hollow in the rocks.

She didn't say anything, just watched him, weighing something. Finally she produced his rifle and knife from beneath some rocks and gave them to him.

"Wake me when it is dark," she said. "We will move then."

Daniel nodded and she curled herself up in the hollow and fell asleep immediately.

The canyon was very dark and deep. Daniel had stumbled several times, but the girl remained silent. Having assumed command, she seemed to have lost her voice. She seemed preoccupied with something. Her eyes were always moving.

She stopped suddenly and motioned him back into a dark corner of the twisting canyon. She followed him, running. Together they pushed themselves into a break in the rock wall. Something of her fear communicated itself to him even though he didn't know what she was hiding from.

"Up there," she whispered urgently, pointing at the canyon wall opposite them. "Kill it."

He looked up, but all he could see was a goat scrambling across the rocks. He hesitated.

"Kill it. Kill it." She was shaking with fear.

He suddenly understood that it was the goat she wanted him to kill. He aimed, started to fire, but it jumped aside. He tried again, but as he tracked it, it changed course again. It was scrambling desperately toward the lip of the canyon. Always it jumped aside just as he was steadying to fire.

The girl was watching with fascinated horror.

Daniel dropped the rifle from his shoulder. The goat stopped immediately and stared down at them. Its red eyes glowed in the night's darkness. It seemed to know it was safe.

Daniel swung the rifle casually on his hip and fired without warning. Dust jumped just above the goat. He worked the bolt and fired again. The goat was running, full out, no longer dodging before each shot. It was moving fast and hard toward the top of the canyon. He fired again but missed. Each of the unsighted shots were very close, but the goat escaped.

Daniel set the rifle down. "It knew just when I was going to fire a shot," he said. He looked at Derl.

"No. No." She seemed to have gained some reassurance from the shots he had fired and the way the goat had run away. "It must have known when I thought you were going to fire. It didn't know when you changed and fooled me." She seemed very pleased that she was the source of the goat's knowledge and not Daniel.

"What was it?" Daniel asked. "Goats aren't that smart."

But she wouldn't answer. The question seemed to have brought something back to her.

"Come with me," she said. "We have to hide now."

She led him into a small side canyon. It was blocked with a huge bush and she knelt down to crawl under it. He followed, recognizing the sharp needles and twisted branches. It was another of those kind.

When she reached the trunk she stopped and waited for him to crawl up next to her. "We have to stay here," she whispered. "The goat will find us anywhere else."

Daniel did not argue. As the night wore on he relaxed and finally fell asleep again.

Daniel woke and Derl clamped her hand across his mouth. The hunters were close now and she concentrated on making the bush conceal them. She could hear thrashing sounds in the brush nearby and an occasional shout.

"There is another one of the things over here!" a voice cried.

She knew it was close, too close. Someone started hacking at her bush. She closed her eyes and focused on the mind of the Therb. She let its feelings come to her and she soothed its rudimentary fears. Someone was hacking at its living source. The pain was almost overwhelming. Fight back. Move branches that ordinarily only moved following the sun. She guided and strengthened the commands of the Therb and was rewarded with a scream of pain from outside. The bush began to sway and thrash violently. The cry of pain changed and became one of fear.

Daniel tried to rise, but she kept him down. She had to concentrate. The distraction broke her hold on the bush and it sagged back into its normal position. The shouting and commotion outside increased and the hacking started again. Someone's face peered through a hole in the bush.

"There they are, both of theeeeaaaaawwwwww."

She glared and the man's face contorted. He jerked forward like a robot and threw himself onto the hacked-off stump of a branch. The attack on the bush stopped.

"Derl! Come out. We won't hurt either of you."

That was Grant. Anyone else she wouldn't have listened to.

"Why?" she called back. "You should kill us both."

"We can't. The Flame wants you both alive."

Derl spat out her disbelief. "Will you prove it," she called. "Will you let me read you?"

Grant hesitated at this request. "All right," he agreed.

He stepped into sight and looked down at them. "He must agree too," Grant said, pointing down at Daniel.

Derl thought quickly. She took the rifle from him and Daniel watched, trusting that she knew best in this situation. She did not explain because there was no time. "He will agree."

Grant relaxed at this promise and he looked at her. Derl concentrated hard. Grant became rigid and then relaxed again.

"Satisfied?" he asked.

She nodded and handed him the rifle.

Grant took it and handed it away behind him. Then he reached down to help her up with his left hand. She gripped it with both of hers and Grant pulled. Suddenly, almost without thought, Grant jerked her forward, turning his head away and swinging his right fist at the same time. Derl's head snapped back. She sagged and collapsed under the blow. There was a fleeting thought as she sank into darkness. Somehow Grant had guessed her intentions—that she had not really been willing to give herself and Daniel to the Flame.

Grant carried the girl on his shoulder. Daniel was dragged along by four of his men. Derbid carried the rifle. Together they approached the ring that would send all of this trouble to the demons. Grant was glad of this.

He motioned and the rifle was thrown into the ring. It disappeared. Daniel was thrown after it, ungently. Derl was last. Grant placed her in the ring gently. He touched the bruise on her face lightly. I hope I did not hurt you badly, he thought, as she vanished. You would have been a good leader—and I was afraid of you.

PART TWO.

In Darkness

Chapter 7.

Robert Stassen sifted through the mountain of paper, deep in the archives of the moon. Each trip the colonial ship returned to Alpha loaded with paper and information, all in a vain attempt to unravel the mystery of the Earth's collapse. It was Stassen's job to see that the paper and information would be of some use this time. But how could he do that?

There was no clue to what had happened. In the fifty years following the Earth's last ship to Alpha there had simply been a crash. The whole civilization on Earth had dissolved into anarchy and apathy. There were no major wars, no evidence of disease or crop failures. People had simply lost the will to work and hold civilization together. There was no explanation.

It was frightening, and this is why the authorities on Alpha insisted that the search for a reason continue. If human civilization could collapse unexpectedly on Earth, then it could happen anywhere. Even on Alpha.

This lunar base was an example of what collapse could mean. Efforts to maintain the integrity of the structure had simply stopped. Leaks had developed and the air had simply drained away, along with the life of the inhabitants.

Stassen shuddered. He could still remember the perfectly preserved bodies and clothes that had been found on his first visit to the base. And no record as to why they had let it happen.

A call from the ship interrupted his thoughts. "The captain wishes to see you," an impersonal voice explained, and Stassen left his work and began his climb up through the levels of the base.

He was shown into the main operations room, where the captain was waiting for him.

"An interesting development," the captain explained. "You wanted us to report when any of the marked equipment left the island."

Stassen was immediately alert. He had wanted to know if any of the new colonists were somehow leaving the island and reaching the mainland. Transmitters had been planted in some special items that were the most likely to be taken along on a boat.

The captain produced a map of the island. He pointed at a dotted line. "This is the plot of one of your items. A rifle. You can see how it has traveled the full length of the island."

"Yes," Stassen answered impatiently, "but the plot ends while still on land. It hasn't left the island yet."

The captain smiled grimly. He produced another map, this time of the mainland. He pointed at a position in the central mountains. "You can see that the plot resumes here, almost a thousand miles from where it left the island. It made the jump instantaneously."

Stassen looked at the two maps. "But that's impossible!"

Bork Dakkett-O, inspector general of the Nuuian Central Council, stepped through the corelink receiver on the planet Earth. Here he was met by Sordin Raddi-Ka, occupation general and production leader of the planet.

The two studied each other in silent hostility. The inspector general's visit had been planned as a surprise, but it obviously wasn't. Nevertheless, he would carry out his instructions to the letter. He did not want a test of power at this moment, so he greeted the occupation general on the picture level. Ideas coursed between the two and could be translated thus:

Bork: "Greetings, brother commander."

Sordin: "What meaning has this?"

Bork: "I come to check your production quota."

Sordin: Humor. "You are most welcome to check my production quota."

Bork: "Thank you."

The undertones of this communication were of hostility and knowing lies. The two were deadly enemies, as were all inspectors general and occupations general. This was the wisdom of the council. The inspectors general were always stronger as individuals but didn't have the power of an occupation army behind them. Thus a balance was maintained.

Bork inspected the great chute that was dumping coal into the corelink transmitter. "Why has production been reduced?"

Sordin: "The natives are most difficult. They die quickly if not treated with care."

Bork: "This will have to be proven."

Sordin: "Good fortune attends us. A new specimen awaits your attention."

The two proceeded to the recruitment center where Daniel Trevor lay stretched on a table. The girl had been quickly hidden by Sordin's people because her discovery would reveal the true reason that production quotas were down.

Sordin: "You notice the health and strength of this specimen. But there is a difference."

Bork: Shock. "The mind structure is different. Is this the case with all of them?"

Sordin: "Yes. An eight-level mind. Information has been prepared for your more perfect understanding."

Bork: Less hostility. "Perhaps there is true cause for your trouble."

Sordin: Hidden satisfaction. "Yes. Certainly."

The inspector general was shown to his sleeping quarters, where he was given a great deal of information on the oddities of the natives. The greater his preoccupation with this the less he would see of the real cause for concern.

Daniel woke in a yellow fog. It was warm and comfortable. He closed his eyes and slept again.

The next time he woke, the fog was gone, replaced by a haze of softness in his mind. Everything seemed just right. He did not feel the cold metal of his cell but he looked at it with slow wonder and touched it. Smooth curved walls rose around him and met above his head. He was on his back looking up at his hand touching the ceiling. Everything was comfortable.

The cell was like the inside of a tin can: a cylinder about ten feet long and four feet high with a metal cap on one end. The other end was blocked by dark, greenish-looking rock.

The cap was moving, opening, and Daniel knew that it was time to get up. He crawled through the opening and into a corridor. Its walls were lined with cells just like his and like bees hatching from a cone, people were crawling out and walking away. Daniel followed. The corridor was long and it entered another larger one. People were everywhere, but they didn't speak. They smiled. Daniel smiled back, but there was a flickered question deep in his mind: *Why am I smiling?*

Ten minutes of walking brought them to the end of the large way. Several large rings were set in the ground at the end of the corridor. People stepped into them and vanished. Daniel knew this was right and he followed.

The corridor was gone and Daniel found himself walking in a large open cavern. Machines and dust were everywhere. Some machines were motionless and he walked to one of these. He had done this many times before—but this was the first time he actually realized it, even in so little a sense as remembering that he had done it before. He climbed into the machine and seated himself, hands on the controls. The machine lurched forward, ripping into the walls of the huge cavern, and pulverizing what it managed to pull away.

Hours passed and the walls shrank back a little. Daniel settled into the pounding routine, which drove away the painful flickerings of doubt. Then he was finished. He did not feel the fatigue that the vibrating machine had given him. His ears were not hurting from the constant roar of the work.

Slowly he walked toward the exit rings. Someone stepped on his foot and he stumbled. He smiled as he climbed to his feet.

He stepped into the exit ring, and his cell walls surrounded him. Food was waiting, and he ate.

Yellow gas poured into the chamber, and Daniel went to sleep.

Chapter 8.

Bork Dakkett-O, inspector general, was a bureaucrat and a good one. He was also a carnivore, nearly seven feet tall and human-looking except for his eyes and the texture of his skin. His skin was a smooth, painted gray. Its feel was like plastic. His eyes were mostly iris, red velvet, surrounding a purple pupil. In the dark a dim light came from them. The blood in his veins was warm and made his skin hot to the touch.

Bork had many things in common with humans, especially brains and a skill for managing others.

He cursed his skill now. It and this forsaken planet would be his undoing. Pacified! Bah! He hissed at the thought. The place was crawling with vermin.

He could not understand how other inspectors general had failed to see and report these things. The idiosyncrasies of the natives. The nature of their resistance to control. The real reasons for the falling off of production. Why had these things never been reported?

He reviewed the contact reports—recorded as they always were in the mind fragment of one of Sordin's brooding eggs. The egg would never hatch, because of the use it had been put to, but the information it held could be viewed with the assurance that it was accurate and could be transferred to another egg when this one grew to term and died on failing to hatch.

The images and information it held flowed out to him, unresisting. The conquest of Earth had been easy. All but a few of the native leaders had been easy to control and the civilization had simply been collapsed around them. The mining of coal and other carbon-complex minerals had proceeded well at first. But the work forces died and had to be continually replaced. Natives had to be left free on the planet's surface in order to breed, and then had to be continually recruited for work in the mines.

There was another disturbing problem. It was becoming more and more difficult to recruit new workers. There was a native resistance in the creatures that had been bred stronger by the constant removal of the weaker. This would have to be investigated.

The whole problem was intriguing as well as dangerous. Sordin, the occupation general, was obviously resourceful. He'd gotten around inspectors general before. How was Bork going to prevent him from doing it again?

Three weeks of intensive effort left Bork frustrated and disturbed. Searching through translated native records he'd been unable to find any reference to telepathy as a recognized tool. Yet the gene factor was .016, and about 1 native in every 4,000 definitely had the ability —although, even in these, it was extraordinarily hard to develop a true talent. Still, a small and significant number did exist. Under ordinary conditions those few should have dominated the life on this planet.

But the records showed otherwise. When the first strike force had arrived on the planet and begun its work, deficients had been living on an equal basis with the talented. Such a thing was an unprecedented event. It was, in fact, considered to be culturally impossible. Planets with an even lower gene factor had been well researched and although they were usually primitive, the normal pattern of domination by the talented was always observed.

In the most primitive cases large groups of deficients always formed around each talented individual. During the early stages there was always violence because crossbreeding with deficients caused the submergence of the telepathic talent in the second generation. This often caused the group to break up for lack of a talented leader. Even after the discovery of inbreeding to perpetuate the talent in the leader's family, trouble was caused by the occasional talented persons born to deficient parents. Since most of the genes involved were recessive there was no way to prevent this from happening. Only after the problem of accidental talent was solved by a steady policy of adoption or extermination at birth did real progress begin on the usual backward world.

Here, something had gone wrong, drastically wrong. Those with talent failed to exert the normal influence.

It was perhaps something he had noticed in the structure of the native mind. He would inquire of the biospecialist what these differences meant. He had to understand the problems of the occupation general before he could make a clear judgment.

Biospecialist: Very nervous. "No, it is not a new strain of bacteria or a trace compound. The difference is in the mind structure itself."

Bork: "Explain."

Biospecialist: "It is the fourth part of their minds: language. All intelligence we know of communicates with the third part: state. Even as you and I. Pictures of things, feelings, colors, sound, motion. The flow of our thought is very simple.

"Example: You order me to produce a document. Picture; yourself. Feeling; compulsion. Picture; myself. Motion; toward yourself. Picture; document.

"I've slowed the thought intentionally so that you could see its components. We do not think in components, but in complete thoughts. This is why it is so difficult to understand these natives. It also explains the impossibility of controlling them properly."

"Example: You order a native to produce a document. Picture; yourself. Formulate; word. Verbalize; word. Hear; word. Reformulate; picture.

"Just to transmit the first portion of your command takes enormous time and must struggle through the language portion of the native's mind. This is naturally difficult and explains the reason native talents have not been able to exert a normal influence. Their strength is buffered by this fourth portion of the mind."

Bork began to perceive the enormous difficulty in commanding in this way. "How terrible. How can they communicate? How can civilization develop? Doesn't this language reduce them below the level of animal?"

Biospecialist: Excited. "Not so. There are compensations. They must think slowly, yes, but how different. Notice these."

Bork glanced at the pile of books in the corner. "Records?"

Biospecialist: More excited. "Not so. Imaginings."

Bork: Unable to comprehend. "Things that have not happened? Will not happen? Cannot happen? What use are these?"

The biospecialist launched into a vast and technical explanation. Bork followed its wider outline. Language was a part of the Human hierarchy of the mind, similar to the ones that Bork already understood: existence, body, and state. It not only existed along with these others, but also it somehow broke down the barriers among them.

This produced an odd sort of communication that was not communication. Fiction: what did not happen. Religion: what should happen, but never did.

Bork understood neither concept perfectly. This did not matter. What was more important was the effect of this language on power and telepathy. This language acted as a fog through which neither could travel perfectly. Drugs were being used to bypass this part of the alien mind and allow the transmittal of instruction and order without a crippling drain on the commanding mind.

There were many implications in this that Bork needed time to work out. He retired from his interview with the biospecialist and returned to a study of records. These, at least, set as they were in the mind fragments of eggs, would not cause pain and stretching to understand unknown things.

The study-of-native-life center was located in the central portion of an upper level of the Nuuian underground complex. Sordin, occupation general, visited the center daily. It was here that his hopes for the future lay. It was here that he was developing the power with which he would one day command the entire Nuuian Empire.

Sordin looked at the female specimen that lay on the table before him. It was the best so far. The mind quivered as he pushed through the perceiving level and began to manipulate the affecting level. There was resistance and he could feel the active will of the native retreating in confusion. It did not know how to foil him and it fell back farther and farther into its self. Only the confusing complexity of the alien mind and a need to keep this one alive kept him from completing the union.

But complete union was not needed. As the doctor had predicted, co-operation came. It was slow and dull-minded, but this didn't bother him. He had to learn. He had to master this technique of co-operation if victory was to be his.

Only one union, as the complete subjugation of a lower form's mind was termed, was perfect; that of the female of his own species. It was this special relationship that made the Nuuians what they were. Not just another intelligent telepathic race, but the masters of older and larger races.

The female Nuuian, like the male, was born with the power to control. But there was an important difference. When a female was overcome it submitted completely, without reservation, while the male would die resisting, or submit only on a qualified basis. Because the females hatched first, their ability matured sooner than the males'. The same situation arose with every batch of eggs: The most powerful female quickly gained control over all other females, and the males were forced to flee. The first male strong enough to overcome the combined strength of all the females would get them all. The rest of the males would be driven away permanently. A few of those outcasts might eventually find a female group left unconquered by its accompanying male hatch. If the wandering male had strength enough, it could win the prize lost in its own hatch.

Sordin mused on this difference. Without this biological quirk, the Nuuian would not have the power to reach through great distances of space. Even the great concentrating effect of the mind rings would be useless without the group mind to power them.

Now, before him, lay another biological quirk. A race with its power prisoned within itself. And he knew what this was. He had experienced this power. For three hundred years he'd kept the secret—the real secret of Earth—from his superiors and the great Nuuian Council.

He felt the native female struggle beneath his control and he brought himself back with a jerk to the contest that he had almost forgotten. A great blast of power surged over him. The native's fear struggled to engulf him. Great currents of undirected energy escaped from her mind and struck down all the others in the shielded room. They stumbled back, cowering, unable to withstand the crushing fear and panic.

Sordin gathered himself. Mercilessly he drove inward and struck at the breathing center. The native shuttered. Its body struggled for breath in vain. Only when it sagged into unconsciousness did Sordin release his hold and settle back exhausted.

The head of the center, Domrel, climbed to his feet, shaking. He rushed to the native and rapidly began restoring it to life.

Sordin: Apologetic. "My concentration wandered. It should never have happened."

Head of the center: Great concern. "Nothing, not even the shielding of this room, could contain the power of that transmission. It may cause trouble with the inspector general." Apology for unthinking criticism. "Of course, only your strength of will saved us all from death."

Mind structure as understood by Nuuian.
(Life structure might be a better term.)

EXISTENCE

1. **PRESENCE**

   This is the universal attraction of all existing things. Expressed in a physical sense this is gravity.

2. **LOCATION**

   This is the universal framework (position of presence in this framework) and is in a physical sense defined by the emptiness of space with distance and direction defined by light. The unchanging speed of light is what makes this framework fixed and definable.

3. **ACTIVITY**

   Characteristic identity of any individual thing as defined by its activity. Character. In a physical sense defined by electromagnetic force and other identifying ("weak") forces.

BODY

4. **MASS**

   This is the momentum and the inertia of any existing thing. Weight, speed, etc., in a physical sense. Body, genes, memory, experience, etc., in a living sense.

5. **SENSE**

   All interaction between one object and all other objects. Physical forces acting upon a living thing. All the incoming data upon which future action might be based.

6. **DESIRE**

   Semivoluntary impulses originated by a living thing (sex, hunger, thirst, territory protection, etc.). All body or biological-preservation impulses dealing with self. Body activity.

STATE

7. EMOTION

Voluntary state of mind (affection, relaxation, excitement, displeasure, etc.). All of these states are generally directed outward, but influential internally.

8. INTENTION

Voluntary direction that future acts will focus on. As in emotion, this does not necessarily promote survival of an individual's body.

9. COMMUNICATION

All impulse and activity directed toward influencing other living things. Gestures, sounds, and most importantly, telepathy.

NOTE: The above is the order as observed by a telepathic mind from the outside. (Presence is detected first, followed by location, etc., communication being detected last.)
To forcibly influence such a mind the order is reversed. (Communication is affected first, followed by intention, etc., with presence being the last.)

Chapter 9.

Bork moved toward the native-life center with a steady purpose. His study of records had been disturbed by the impact of a transmission he didn't understand. It had been similar to a group probe, but without direction or purpose, unless the broadcast of panic might serve some purpose. Perhaps it was something used to keep the aboveground natives away from the complex. The alien nature of the broadcast made this plausible, and he was determined to find out how it had been amplified to such strength.

The technicians and guards he met on the way seemed to shrink back from him. Their minds were carefully guarded with thoughts of no consequence.

Passing through the outer section of the native-life center, Bork noticed a heavy quality in the air. The Nuuian workers in the area seemed reluctant even to exchange courtesies with him. As he approached the laboratory section a frightened guard stepped into his way.

Bork was taken by surprise. "What is the meaning of this!"

The thought was more of a command to step aside than a question. The lowly guard nearly collapsed under the heavy probe. Bork's power was so great that the guard moved aside involuntarily, his fist still clenching and unclenching in warning. Bork ignored the silent message.

He pushed into the shielded laboratory section, and something intangible in the air made him freeze. It was a very strong primitive transmission, completely out of control and obviously alien and human-native in character. What was frightening was that there was no message—no content in the transmission. It was just a background wash of feeble impulses.

Bork snapped himself away from the currents of white nothing and blocked them. There was no direction in them, no attempt to break down his barriers, and he realized suddenly that he was not in immediate danger of death.

The head of the center hurriedly closed the shielded door to the outside.

Bork: Furious. "What is going on here? What is this?"

The head of the center quivered under the questioning. No individual was strong enough to withstand an inspector general, and the head of the center fervently hoped that Bork would not lose control and begin to extract information forcibly. There was too much to hide.

There was no way the head of the center could successfully lie to the inspector general, so the head of the center decided to tell the truth in a partial way.

Head of the center: Calm. "Let us step out beyond the shielding where it will be possible to converse comfortably."

Once outside, with the thick iron door closed behind them, the oppressive atmosphere lifted and they were both able to relax a little.

Bork: Dangerous. "Why wasn't there mention of the power of these natives in any of the reports sent me?"

Head of the center: Honest. "This is a very exceptional case, the result of experimentation."

Bork: Interested. "How is that?"

Head of the center: Greater honesty. "It is part of the occupation general's program to solve the native-control problem. He feels that if natives can be made to control other natives, then the mortality rate will decrease and we can increase production."

Bork: Understanding. "This is good. But how was such power obtained? Isn't it dangerous?"

Head of the center: "We already use native transmitters to buffer the instructions we send to the workers. It keeps the workers alive longer, but the buffers die quickly. This native is the result of a breeding experiment to overcome the problem."

Bork: Great concern. "This is a natural product? There was no mechanical amplification?"

Head of the center: Unworried. "There is nothing to fear from these natives. This case is an isolated phenomenon, but even with such power the native is unable to resist our control."

Bork: Unconvinced. "Even under control this experiment represents too much of a danger. I will speak with the occupation general and order the specimen destroyed."

Head of the center: Pleading. "The situation is under control. You have never had direct contact with these natives before. I must demonstrate what it is like so you will understand."

The head of the center led Bork back into the shielded lab section. From behind a one-way glass Bork got his first good look at the human female. It seemed calm now and there was no detectable transmission.

Bork: Puzzled. "Why doesn't it attack?"

Head of the center: "It is unable to. It can barely detect the first level of our existence (existence$_1$ = presence). Because we lack language, it is unable to distinguish us from any other life form without going beyond presence. This it hasn't learned to do except in the case of a few native plants and fellow humans. Also it is completely unable to defend itself. It has no concept of directionalizing its power, but broadcasts or defends over the entire sphere—in all directions."

Bork tested what the head of the center told him. It was true. The native girl's mind was completely open. He could descend through all perceiving levels without even arousing the creature. It was only when he began to probe the affecting levels that it began to react. Bork backed away, unwilling to provoke the violent-fear broadcast he could feel was forming.

Bork: Curious. "How can it broadcast so powerfully to a deep body-affecting area without going through upper levels?"

Head of the center: Excited. "You noticed. Only the occupation general and biospecialist have remarked on this ability before yourself. It is a peculiarity of the language." He showed Bork a crude mental diagram. "Notice our mind structure. Its layers are like the skins of an onion. Lower layers cannot be entered without passing through all the higher layers. Notice the human mind structure. The existence, body, and state layers are similar to ours, but the additional layer of language interlaces them all. It is like a tree rotten with termites. The layers are there, but wormholes and tunnels lead to and fro through them all. This is why they instinctively try to defend the entire sphere. A skillful intelligence (any Nuuian) can follow any of these tunnels (once he has learned the trick) and immediately reach the deepest controlling layers."

Bork was taken aback by this absorbing and graphic explanation. He could suddenly understand why the human was defenseless despite its power and why the head of the center saw no danger in this power.

Bork retired to privacy to consider all he had learned. This was a fascinating race. He would have to recommend that specimens be transported to the Central Council for study. They were unique in his experience. And the power. If it could somehow be put to use!

Chapter 10.

Three levels below Inspector General Bork's quarters, an over-worked Nuuian technician puzzled over a piece of native equipment he was supposed to examine. He hadn't seen anything like it since the early days of the occupation. He could understand why Sordin, the occupation general, wanted to keep this equipment secret. No outsider was to know that the human population on this planet had another source. This knowledge was Sordin's trump card in the terrible game of power that he was playing.

The technician understood these things and he knew that it would be his death if the inspector general learned about them from him. He turned up the shielding on the laboratory to make sure that no stray thoughts escaped while his attention was on the equipment.

The piece itself seemed of little importance. But it wasn't altogether like the simple weapons of the early occupation, and he decided to make an extra-thorough examination.

The X-ray and radio-diffraction prints revealed a number of small defects in the rifle's metallic structure. The technician noted these for later examination.

When he was through with his other work, he returned to the small anomalies. There was nothing unusual about them. A touch of radiation, perhaps. This he would have passed over except for a thought that suddenly struck him. The general technique of the metalwork in the rest of the rifle was too good to allow for accidental defects. The spots themselves revealed nothing, but he felt that his suspicion was firm enough to report, and he did so.

Two hundred fifty thousand miles away, buried deep in a crater on the moon, a faint signal faltered for a moment and then stopped.

"Captain!" the duty officer called over his shoulder. "Something has happened to the signal."

Looking over the blank screen, the captain nodded grimly. He summoned Robert Stassen, the colonial officer, and pointed out the change. "They must have examined the rifle in some way, destroying the transmitter."

Stassen agreed with this judgment. "The questions are: Who made the examination? What kind of civilization exists down there? How could it have remained hidden from us for three hundred years?"

The captain had an answer to the last of these questions. "By examining the rifle's signal we have been able to trace its movements through almost six miles of underground tunnel. It was almost five hundred feet below the surface when the signal stopped."

Stassen looked at the captain. "We will have to go down, examine the place more closely."

The captain shook his head. "No, sir. The colony is your responsibility, but the ship is mine. The ship will not venture closer to Earth than it is now. Too much depends on our returning, even with only what little information we have now."

Stassen accepted this. But he was going to get men down to that spot somehow.

Chapter 11.

Daniel Trevor's body moved without effort. It worked and slept and ate. Time did not seem to pass. In flashes and snatches Daniel sensed this. But he was struggling with something else. A soft and comfortable darkness enveloped him. It yielded to the touch, but flowed in again, forever pressing down.

It is hard to describe what happened, because Daniel himself hardly understood the internal construction that made him struggle. He had learned one simple trick very early in life, and that was what he clung to now: No matter how narrow the range of choice, there was always room for *him*. To die or be captured. To eat or go without. He never submitted to a choice—he always made it as an act of policy in his life. Even submission, if he chose it, *must* be an active choice.

Instead of dragging forward, he was always pursuing a line he actively visualized deep inside. It really existed for him—this thin and trembling line. And at the forward end of this line was a small pocket of room—the range of choice and direction open to him. All his life he'd fought with every exertion of his will to expand this sense of room in himself. To him, it was life itself. In a very real way, it had been "loss of room" that had caused him to become a killer. Reading a news article had brought the size of his and his father's world crashing down into almost nothing. He *had* to kill.

And now it was the same, only worse. There was nothing to kill, only comfortable, crushing blackness. There was nothing in the whole of his mind but rage and a dark maelstrom of struggle. This was his sole choice: to struggle forward against the black—to burn inside until the fire freed or destroyed him.

Exhaustion slowly became the color of his sight. And just as gradually as his vision changed, he felt something breaking—not in the darkness. In him. The most terrible pain—and through the crack came a red and molten substance. Like lava, it filled the room around him and slowly pressed outward. The blackness sizzled in mindless, unfeeling resistance. It burned and charred with almost audible sound. It filled everything with a foul reek.

Daniel choked and struck out. His hand and arm smashed against steel. They began to bleed freely and Daniel was thrown forward. His face crashed against unbreakable glass. For just the flash of a second he had a picture of what was around him: a huge machine. He was tangled in the controls, alone. Then the flash was gone.

There was another. This time walking, stepping into a metal ring. A surge of motion. Smooth steel. The inside of a tin can.

Flashes came with increasing swiftness. Even as the yellow gas sprayed in around him and brought more of the comfort he was fighting against, he knew he was winning. Exhaustion was his positive guide. There was less of it. The effort to break out was less each time.

Only, in this, Daniel was wrong. It was his strength that increased. There was no weakness in the dark and fuzzy grip. It was simply no longer enough.

The days got longer. Each morning the effects of the yellow gas lessened and his mind became clear sooner. This could have been a fatal process, but he guarded himself. He was careful to imitate the people around him, always moving slowly and keeping his face blank. At the same time, he had to take up the conscious operation of his machine. This was difficult, for when he was fully alert all knowledge of it seemed to vanish from his mind.

Once, as he fumbled inexpertly with the controls, a blank-eyed guard had wandered in his direction. Somehow he had managed to keep the machine pressed forward, grinding against stone, and the guard had passed.

After that Daniel had concentrated on the machine and everything about it. It was fifteen feet high, fifteen feet wide in front, slightly less in the rear, and thirty feet long. A mass of grinding blades swirled at the front of the machine and each time he rammed it forward it tore away great chunks of black rock. The black rock disappeared into a hole at the center of the grinding blades and never came out again. Where did the rock go? He gradually reasoned that there must be an exit ring at the center of the machine.

Here was a possible means of escape. There was room enough to crawl inside the machine, but this would have attracted attention.

And he wasn't sure he wanted to be dumped into a stamping mill or some other equally fatal ore-processing equipment.

A better chance lay in developing an understanding of the rings themselves and how they worked. Daniel was personally familiar with only four sets. The one inside his cell he termed a "receiver." It brought him there but he couldn't exit the same way. Similar "receivers" existed everywhere in the mine and he observed how new shifts of workers arrived through them.

"Sending" rings were larger. There were many of these in the mine but no matter which you entered, it always sent you to the same cell. The other set of "senders" lay at terminal points in the prison tunnel system. These would only send him to the mine, but he'd noticed that other prisoners didn't arrive in the same cavern. Somehow the rings were personalized. They recognized who you were and sent you where you belonged.

Each day as he passed through, he would try to examine them a little more closely, but there was nothing to see. There were no wires or motors—no connection to any power source he could see.

He might have been content to study this problem for some time if something shocking hadn't come along to make him act immediately.

Bork finally arranged time enough to visit the mines and to see some of the work actually under way. He looked at the machines and the great efficiency, but what he was really searching for was evidence of the great power he'd noticed in the female native. He wanted to make sure that she was an exception.

The potential involved in such power was beginning to impress him. Two or three natives like the one he'd seen, properly united with a Nuuian mind, would be unstoppable. It would have the power of a large mind-union, but would not be handicapped by the limited mobility of the Nuuian female. The human natives would not be tied for hundreds of years to egg clutches, nor would they be affected by threats to an egg clutch. They could travel with the complete freedom of a Nuuian male.

Bork began to realize the danger of his situation. If the suspicions he had became known to Sordin, the occupation general, and if they were true, then Bork would never return to the Council from this inspection. There would be an accident and Sordin would take his chances on the inspector general who would be sent to replace him.

He forced this speculation from his mind and concentrated on inspecting the working machinery of the mine. It was important that he continue the appearance of normal inspection. The organic-mineral production was the usual concern of an inspector general, and he would continue to make it one of his. But in doing so he would also be looking at natives whenever the chance arose.

Bork finished his inspection of the mines with some relief. No-where had he seen evidence of unusual native power. The buffer natives, used to control the workers, were all of a low level. Their minds already were showing disintegration at the constant Nuuian control. This cheered him. So long as the native mind refused proper union there was little problem. The danger was that Sordin's breed-ing experiments would somehow overcome this. After all, the occu-pation general had been in control of this planet for more than three hundred years. What had he done in all that time aside from mine coal?

Daniel slumped down in the seat of his machine. He saw but couldn't believe. Only the terrible closed-in feeling that rolled over him *was* real—so real that he became almost physically ill.

Somehow he restrained his urge to leap from the machine and strangle the gray alien. Instead, Daniel endured the smothering pres-ence and held tight to cold steel.

Finally the alien passed beyond his sight. Its red eyes had never once turned to look at him, yet Daniel had felt at every instant the pressure of cold awareness. And he had resisted that awareness—pushing it back—rejecting it. And as he rejected it he came to realize that *it* had once held him captive—not yellow gas, not other humans, but a gray, dipped-in-paint thing with so much arrogance and force that it could swallow people into its will.

For a long minute Daniel sat staring into blankness. The people around him ceased to exist in his eyes. They became faceless tools of a force he trembled with eagerness to attack. Or was it fear he trem-bled with and escape he yearned for? For seconds he tipped on the balance, then a semblance of reason returned to his mind. The black hate shrank away and he realized that he could not fight so es-tablished a force alone. He must escape. Now. Immediately.

Still, he hesitated, wisely letting his panic subside. It was replaced by a calmer, but just as firm, resolution.

He let the shift end and joined himself to the mindless surge of people making toward exit rings. He ducked aside at the last moment. In the shadow of one of the great machines he waited until the great underground hall was empty. Only a handful of slack-faced guards remained. Then an incoming surge of workers began.

Daniel ran among them, moving upslope. There had to be an opening to this mine—an exit that didn't involve rings. It was out such an exit Daniel hoped to escape, and uphill was the most likely direction. He ran and walked for twenty full minutes until he finally came to a narrowing down of the mine. But instead of an opening there was a single machine working to open up more room.

Confronted with this, Daniel turned back. As he ran downslope, he wondered how long it would take for the ring-and-prison system to notice that he was no longer in his cell. As if in answer, a guard turned slowly and looked at him as he ran by. Daniel slowed to a walk, hoping this would reassure the guard. It didn't. The guard began to follow. Something weak brushed against his mind and retreated in confusion.

Daniel ran. Desperation brought a snap of clear thinking. He ducked between two machines, climbed into the one on his right, grabbed the driver, and tossed him out. In a second or two *he* was the calm, dull-minded, and rightful driver of that machine.

The guy he'd thrown out just stood there, confused, and looked up at him; little tears were forming in the ex-driver's foggy eyes. Daniel ignored the silent pleading, but he shivered and felt a little sick when the dumb guards grabbed ahold of the poor guy and started pounding on him. They didn't pound long, but when they were through the man was no longer moving. He was never going to move again.

The guards dragged the body away and dumped it into a ring. When it was gone they resumed their mindless patrolling. In the time it took them to do that Daniel had made up his mind. With a quick shifting of gears, he backed his machine out of line and headed it in the direction in which he wanted to go. One of the guards was trudging along in front of him. Daniel did not go out of his way to miss the guard, and in seconds bits of that guard were on their way to the blast furnace, the coal-sorting room, or wherever the machine's internal ring sent them.

After that it was easy. Daniel just kept driving. He passed hundreds of machines and quite a few guards. The guards would look up at him and step out of the way, but for some reason they didn't try to stop him. Maybe it was because he looked like he was going somewhere. Eventually he found out.

The line of working machines finally ended. The mine was now a huge cavern, apparently worked clean from this point on. But there was still plenty of activity. All along the edge of the cavern, on his right where the rings were, he could see scores of broken-down machines. They were literally swarming with lethargic repairmen. Occasionally he would pass a machine clanking past on its way back to the work line. The driver might look dully at him, but otherwise he was ignored. Just another machine needing repair.

The steady downslope ended abruptly and so did the line of machines being repaired. The overhead lighting also ended, along with Daniel's good luck. A guard was standing right in front of him, motioning dully toward an empty spot in the line and a waiting repair crew.

The machine, already in high, was zooming along at six miles an hour, so Daniel just gritted his teeth and aimed it straight ahead. The guard just stood there, watching as the machine's bulk loomed over him. It finally penetrated that the machine wasn't going to turn. The guard's mouth dropped open and he stumbled out of the way.

Looking back, Daniel saw the guard gesticulating madly, his face contorted. When this expression of will failed to stop the machine the guard started after him. Nearby workers laid down their tools carefully and also began to follow.

It was getting darker and since he couldn't see ahead, Daniel kept his eyes on the slowly growing crowd behind him. He jammed the accelerator to the floor and locked it there. Then he crawled out of the cab to defend the rear of the machine. The guard was the first to catch up and he clambered up the rungs on the machine's back as if expecting Daniel to help him up. Instead, he got a shove and a ten-foot tumble to the ground. Things began to happen faster when the crowd was alerted that the machine contained a hostile driver and not merely a stupid one.

The guard scrambled back to his feet, bruises and broken bones unnoticed. Six or seven workers were right behind and closing fast—fast for them, anyway. Daniel held to his station on the back of the machine and kicked them down as fast as they tried to climb up. In the increasing darkness he failed to notice that only half of the workers were trying to climb up at him the easy way.

The first hint of trouble came when he noticed that the machine's engine was winding down. He raced back to the cab. The guard and one worker were there already. Bending over to get back into the cab, Daniel noticed several others slowly climbing up the steep sides of the machine.

As he was staring down at these climbers, the worker in the cab clutched stiffly at his throat.

Daniel brushed the man's arm away and smashed him in the face with a fist. A broken nose and a bloody face didn't bother the man at all, and he was grabbing at Daniel's throat again. This kind of single-mindedness Daniel could do without. He grabbed the man's outstretched arms and hurled him from the cab. Daniel was through fooling around.

The guard was more difficult, but Daniel was able to fend him off with one hand while he restarted the engine with the other. With the machine moving again he was able to devote his full attention to the guard. He knocked in the man's ribs and was about to test his head against a door beam when the machine plowed into a pile of rubble and came to a bone-shaking stop.

Daniel let go of the guard and flicked at the switches on the machine's control panel. Lights flooded on and the darkness disappeared. The mine had shrunk down to a narrow corridor and if he wanted to go farther he would have to drive manually. The guard continued to struggle and an ever-increasing number of workers worked at ripping away Daniel's clothes and pulling him out of the cab. He yanked on the steering and the machine lurched to the side and forward. Someone tried to scratch out his eye, and Daniel gave up trying to watch where he was going. He kicked and pushed, felt someone give way, and heard a scream as a body was ground between the machine's tread and the walls of rock closing in on them.

For a moment Daniel was free to look ahead and he could see that the tunnel ended, blocked by a slide or a cave-in. He managed to downshift and push the guard out of the cab at the same time. Then it was just a matter of fighting off the arms and legs until he couldn't move any longer. Only the fact that they were foolishly pulling on him from both sides kept him from losing his grip on the controls.

The machine moved ahead slowly, pushed into the rubble of the cave-in, and began to eat its way through. An avalanche of rock thundered down, filling the cab with choking dust. The machine continued to move. Suddenly, Daniel was alone in the cab—all the hands holding him had been jerked brutally away.

He took a deep breath and wiped a little of the blood away from his eyes. He was still alive, and they weren't. They had all been pulled outside by the closing walls and cascading rock. For a minute all he could do was smile; then a screeching, grating noise turned his hair into needles. His whole body quivered and stiffened as he watched sharp rocks etching furrows in the sloping armor glass only inches from his face.

More rubble poured in through the open doors as the machine inched its way forward. There was a terrible rending sound as the right- and then the left-hand doors were torn away. The dust was blinding. The screeching sound of rocks against glass and steel lessened a little and Daniel realized that the sound was going away only because he was choking to death. There wasn't any air—only a thick mixture of dust and grit. And all of this was trying to get into his throat. He was doing his best to help it, gasping, sucking, trying uncontrollably to draw it all in. A final gasping cough was almost the last sound he ever made.

The machine paused in its steady grinding progress, then lurched free. A current of cold air flowed into the cab and he took deep, shuddering breaths. He coughed and choked, trying to clear and moisten his throat.

His breathing eased. He shut off the machine's engine with his last strength, then slumped forward—down onto the rock-cluttered floor of the cab. His mind faded toward unconsciousness, but it clung for a moment, savoring the air and the ideas of living and waking up again.

Chapter 12.

The world was filled with lights and colors, growing, changing, and draining away. Derl was learning slowly and painfully which colors were safe and which she must run away from.

The white was safe and meant they were only looking or wanted to talk. The yellow was deeper and she could stay if she were careful. She could watch it and see herself bending and doing what it wanted. But it wasn't her somehow, just something else.

The orange frightened her, but she could still stay. She could force herself to stay. The feelings weren't her. The anger and sadness, laughing and tears. She had to feel them, but they weren't her. She wouldn't let them be.

But the red and the purple and the black. She couldn't stay for these. She ran and stayed away. They tried to make her come out, but she wouldn't. There was a place she could hide, a place they couldn't find her, and it made them mad. She could tell it, feel it through the knives of cutting light that pushed through her. They could never have her all.

Sordin stood by unsatisfied. The elusive but necessary quality of union was missing. The native could be used. It could be made to do this or that, its enormous power could even be directed, but the quality was missing. It would never quite be an extension of one's self, like a true union with the Nuuian female. Herein lay the danger. If the native was to remain just a tool, then it could be anyone's tool. He could not weld it to himself, as he had hoped. Without this insurance he hesitated to undertake so desperate an action as revolt against the whole Nuuian Empire. No, not revolt. He was not interested in revolt. What he intended was conquest. The once and forever grasping of all the scattered and misused group minds of the race.

The race's destiny would never be full until one mind controlled all power—even if only for the short time between hatchings.

Sordin had never believed in the artificial and stifling separation of male and female as imposed by the Council. He had never sanctioned the controlled breeding—the assignment of female group minds only to the males who would shortly pass beyond. The vast bulk of group minds were wasted in the sterile work of operating rings.

This he would change—using mechanical transportation as other races did.

Everything he would change, if only there were some solution to the human problem. Such an opportunity as he was afforded could not be allowed to slip away.

Bork, inspector general, was exhausted by frustration and the inability to grasp the missing piece. His search had been complete, but also it had been unrewarding. In this respect, there was no solution, but as he rested he composed his mind and began the dangerous but necessary process of probing.

The inspector general is blessed with certain advantages over the ordinary Nuuian, and one of these is the ability to probe the state of others without detection. The danger in this lies in having to stretch one's self over distance without the aid of ring or group mind. If discovered in such an attitude, he would be vulnerable to attack, even of only one mind. He could only count on the fear in which he was held. No one would dare probe at an inspector general who had retired to privacy.

It was thus that he stumbled upon the plot of ultimate destruction, not directly, but through an event of lesser importance that was presently disturbing several minds of the occupation force.

A human had escaped from the mines. He detected this communication along with the impulse that the information would be very dangerous if it should reach the inspector general and should at all costs be kept from off-worlders.

Bork learned as much as he could, holding back fury at the reference to himself as an off-worlder.

The human had escaped despite the effects of drugs and the use of an actual mind group to attack. The latter had failed because the lower levels of the human's mind had ceased to exist—or at least had become inaccessible to the mind group. Nothing could be detected of the human except its presence and location. Nothing else was visible.

But why would they want to hide this from him? Bork couldn't understand. They should show it to him as a case of the problems they faced with human minds. Then he detected the awful truth. It wasn't the phenomenon they wanted to hide, but something about the origin of this particular human. He had not been born on Earth.

Bork could not understand the implications of this immediately, but he was outraged at the attempt to hide such knowledge, not only from him, but from the Council as well!

He withdrew his probe and armed himself. This was something he rarely did. Weapons were normally of little use in a contest of minds. But with surprise, it could be used.

He went directly toward the native-life center. It was here that he realized the greatest and most unknown dangers to himself lay. He passed through the clerical sections without acknowledging the few startled greetings that came his way. The guard by the shielded laboratory started to step into Bork's path but died before he could complete his motion. Bork paused only long enough to retrieve the guard's weapon, then he pushed through the shield door and into the laboratory.

There were other Nuuians in the lab, but Sordin, the occupation general, was not there. This was bad, for Bork had hoped to kill him and break opposition quickly.

The head of the center was occupied with the native, and the head's two assistants were turning to face the intruder. Bork shot them instantly, and their deaths warned the head of the center. Suddenly Bork felt a crushing weight on his mind and realized that he was engaged in a fight for his life.

Derl co-operated completely with the direction given her by the head of the center. The mind she enveloped and began to crush was stronger than any of those she had been instructed to crush before. It reacted with sharp blows and could push her back at any point, but not on the full surface of her attack. She had killed her earlier tests easily, and resistance of this sort confused her. The impact of her attack was less than it could have been.

She pushed deeper, reaching for the body centers that would end her opponent's life.

Bork felt his hands relaxing and the weapons slipping from his grasp. He knew what was happening. He struggled desperately for control and for a few seconds resisted the advances being made. But he could tell that resistance would fail. He must find some other way. His strength alone would not save him.

He had to attack—to reach his real opponent, the head of the center. The only way he could do this was through the native. He abandoned resistance and plunged into the strange and whirling mind of the alien. Down Bork went through the unblocked and confusing channels of its language. Bork could feel his body go slack and slump to the ground, but he ignored this. He could feel the crushing weight closing around his heart, but he couldn't think of this. He had to go on.

She was almost there. Derl could feel the pulse slowing. She could stop it at any time. The head of the center's urgent instructions compelled her to kill. But there was hesitation and the watching part of her discovered its first weapon. She could choose her master—she could let through the subtle voice of this new mind, or she could kill it and continue in her slavery to the first.

The push of her hidden self was so small, but its effect was great. The power and direction of her furious attack dissolved. The head of the center detected the change but was powerless. He had instructed her too well in the techniques of sudden death and now they were turned on him. Desperately he tried to kill her. He realized that it was no power of the inspector general's that had effected this change. He tried to kill her, but his heart stopped too soon. His body jerked once and then he was dead.

Bork recovered rapidly from his struggle and it was well that he did. He moved rapidly to free the native from the experimental apparatus enmeshing it and while he worked at the straps he went over in his mind the things he would have to do to escape alive. For the moment he was safe inside the lab but his safety would last only so long as the mental screening around the lab kept his people on the outside from knowing what had happened.

To stay and hide in the laboratory was folly. Even the native's great strength would not protect him from a well-co-ordinated attack by several of Sordin's stronger people. His only chance of living was to reach the main transfer ring and get off the planet. He had to get through it, or get a message through it for help. He must do this or his death would mean the whole Nuuian Empire would be endangered by the revolt Sordin was forming here.

Alone he could not push the message across so much space. But with the native's help he might be able to capture the main sending ring's mind group. With this added power he could escape, send a message, or perhaps even wield enough strength to fight Sordin on his own home ground. With these thoughts Bork finished unbinding the native and forced it to move with him.

Walking was a strange sensation for Derl. She had been strapped down for so long that her legs were sadly weakened. There was pain in them but this she was forced to ignore.

Already she was glad of her choice. She let over all the efforts of her function to the mind that was compelling her and concentrated on watching and learning from the newness that was flooding in on her.

Always she had been able to sense the presence of others, just as she had been able to find Daniel on the seaweed islet. But in the swirl of Nuuian minds and bodies around her now she was learning something new. The presence could be defined—she could see it as place and distance. And deeper, she could sense the strengths and weaknesses of it—the patterns of its thought. And yet deeper, the body and its functioning and flowing. Seeing all of this was not new to her—it was being able to focus on a small area and not see everything at once. It was like seeing rhythm and melody and lyrics coming out separately for the first time in music. She was able to see them coming out and going back together to make a whole thing.

This new seeing she could not reconcile with the sights of her eyes and the sounds of her ears. In the confusion of her senses she tended to bump into and stumble over objects. Bork took her in hand more firmly and forced the physical world into her sight.

Unresistingly she was moving down long passageways. Nuuian minds and bodies fled before her. She could see them moving through walls and earth, and yet they were not there. The walls and floors took their places and she was dizzy trying to see with two minds at once.

It was hard not to close her eyes and see only with the new sense. But she had no choice. To move she must feel and see the realness of nonlife. She was forced to do this. And she moved, always. This was the most important thing. Move, move, never stop.

Bork kept moving. He realized that there was nowhere he could hide, but there were places where he would be physically safe for short periods of time. He used the native continually to search ahead, never risking his own mind in a probe. But always this would cause delay. The native's mind and body would lose contact and she would stumble into walls or fall to the ground. He had to be careful. He could not risk disabling it or making it become immobile. This was his one great advantage over Sordin. He and the native were mobile, while the mind groups he would have to fight could not move.

No one tried to block their way. The areas they approached cleared themselves of occupants faster than Bork could get the native to move. Bork was not fooled by this lack of resistance, but he was determined to take advantage of it by heading straight for the communication center and the ring that could send him down to the main transfer ring and then from there, off the planet.

He soon discovered why no one was trying to stop him. The way to the communication center was blocked by a dead-weight panel. The panel weighed several tons and it completely sealed the corridor. It was a one-way mechanism that couldn't be removed even with the co-operation of the people on the other side. Such panels were ancient emergency measures to ensure the safety of vital areas, even when they were under attack by stronger mental forces.

Bork was furious. Sordin was making use of medieval devices that hadn't been used since the days when Nuuian fought Nuuian. But what else?

Bork discontinued his fury. Since the block could not be moved except by great manual effort or by blasting, it was useless to waste more time.

He turned back and headed for the central power supply. This time he had the wisdom not to repeat his mistake. With the help of the native's power Bork reached ahead and was able to prevent anyone in the power room from closing off that section.

When he was within sight of the entrance to the power room, the lights suddenly dimmed. Someone was trying to down the power. Bork had been so preoccupied with keeping the way open that he had failed to see this move. Quickly, he reached out with all the power at his disposal and put an end to it. The lights continued to flicker and Bork knew he would have to hurry.

Inside the power room everyone was either dead or unconscious. Bodies clung to controls or reached out desperately for switches they would never touch. This was a small comfort because one of them had managed to partially destroy the power control panel before dying. It was melted and fused in several places.

Bork hurried because time was getting short. He could already feel the probing of a group mind. All it needed was a little more time to organize. Then, if it found him, he wouldn't stand a chance—he was still too close to it to resist effectively. He had to get away fast.

Thinking frantically, Bork remembered the escape incident in the mine that had triggered his resolve. Perhaps those very mines would be his salvation now. He knew that there were several abandoned sections of the mine. If he could reach one of them he would be safe for a time. They could never move a group mind close enough to him.

Bork studied the sending rings in the power section. He changed the field settings, disconnecting the sending rings from the group mind that usually operated them. He gripped the native and together they stepped into the ring. Using a whipsaw effect, he pushed her through and then had her drag him after her. Together they made the jump, where alone, he would have been helpless to escape.

There was nothing but darkness at emergence. There was a stale smell of dead air. Bork gripped the native carefully before commanding her to step out into the pitch darkness all around them. The ground was level and safe. He followed the native.

Here in the dark emptiness he would be safe to think and plan—and he would have the native to defend himself with.

Chapter 13.

The darkness of night was still there when Daniel woke up. Only a tiny light showed in the cab of the great machine, filling it with a soft luminescence. It was a nice light to wake up to and it eased the buzzing in his head and the stiffness in his body. It was good to be alive, even if you felt sore and your stomach was empty.

Daniel wormed his way out of the cab and stretched. The broad back of the machine was littered with broken rock and he moved his feet carefully, brushing some of the rubble over the side. The sound of it hitting the ground stopped him short. There was an echo. He was still underground. It was something he should have noticed right away. The absolute absence of light from above, or the dank stillness of the air should have told him.

Daniel's thoughts became grave as he considered the implications of the fact. There was no telling how big this new chamber was, but from the echo he could estimate that it was at least as large as the one from which he had escaped.

With sudden haste Daniel began to clear away the rock from the back of the machine and from inside the cab. If this chamber was an abandoned part of the mine, then there might still be rings in it. And if there were rings in here, then he wasn't safe or free yet.

When he turned on the forward running lights his fears were confirmed. He didn't know what it took to destroy a ring but if anything could, it would be the crushing weight of the giant mining machine. He started it up and proceeded to do his best, riding one of the treads over the metal framework of the nearest ring, crushing it flat. For good measure he pivoted on the spot and then backed away to inspect the damage. He noticed with satisfaction that there was nothing much left.

Looking ahead Daniel could see that a line of rings stretched out into the darkness. He drove on, crushing them as he passed and hoping that they might eventually lead him to the end of the mine and to the surface.

The open expanse of empty darkness had an unsettling effect on Bork. As the uneventful hours passed he began to cast about for something to keep his mind alert. This, he discovered, would be the perfect time to inspect the powers and potentials of his unwilling helpmate. There were certain aspects of the mind that he wanted to look into more closely.

Bork found the memories unusually dull. This female human seemed to have spent its entire early life grubbing for food. But that was to be expected of a lower life form.

No. There was something else there. Something important! In some of the clearest of its memories the native seemed to be watching the landing of some kind of ship. Bork studied these memories carefully, wanting to learn as much as he could about the ship and why it was landing. But he was disappointed. There was something peculiar about the way the native girl remembered these things. The pictures and sensations she had recorded were unnaturally colored. It was almost as if the girl had mixed dream images with the real impressions of her senses!

This brought to mind something that the biospecialist had told him: the frequency with which unreality crept into many of the native recordings.

Did this unreality extend even into their own memories? Bork could not believe this, and yet he was finding himself more and more enmeshed in vivid sensations that could not be real. How could the native function when the very basis of its memory experience was so confused? How could he, Bork, distinguish the differences when the native itself couldn't?

Bork withdrew and pondered the unusualness of this. There must be some aspect of language that encouraged this. Would prolonged study of such minds affect the one who studied them?

The implications of this question were disturbing. Suddenly the stature of the human race and what was happening on this planet took on a different value. Everything about the Nuuian mind and the Empire they had built was based on absolutes. Knowledge and reality were absolute. There was no fiction or question—only facts. Power and your position in power were absolutes, almost from the day of the hatching. Nothing could change your destiny or what you were fated to be.

But here Bork felt the slipperiness of a trap. Could anything destroy a mechanism of power and control as carefully built and developed as the Nuuian Empire?

The upheaval in Bork's mind caused him to withdraw farther within himself. He must consider this, he must find a solution. But he must stay alert and alive at the same time.

He reached a compromise with himself. He would concentrate most of his effort on discovering a solution to this new question, but he would retain enough control of the native to serve him as a warning. She would detect the approach of any danger and draw him out to defend himself.

Derl found herself alone and her mind free for virtually the first time since her capture. She wasn't entirely free, of course, and she concentrated on watching just as she had been instructed. But there was a difference. She was using her own mind and the new senses on her own part, not as an extension of someone else's will.

She could sense the distant activity of minds that were at this very minute engaged in search for her and her master. But extreme distance made them appear as mere dots, not the disks and full spheres she had become used to seeing. Somehow she knew that while she could observe them at this distance, they could not see or locate her.

Perhaps this was because the darkness and silence of the mine made it easier for her to use her new sense. Or perhaps it was because she was more powerful and could see farther. This thought pleased her, then made her uneasy. She was not supposed to think, just watch.

But she did think, and it was fun. She reveled in the sense of being uncontained. She felt like exploding. But she didn't. She was held as a fish on a line, with freedom to move but not to escape.

Her new sense wasn't really new. But it was different. They had somehow changed it, or maybe she just learned to imitate them. Before it had just been blurs and vagueness, but now it was like colors and directions, shapes and sizes, powers and patterns.

She wanted to use it all and test herself, and she cast about for a way. The minds in the distance were too far away, but there was something closer. It was a little mind, and not so many colors, but it was near and she could use it. It was only a few hundred feet away, and up, directly above her. A small burrowing animal in the rocks of the mine's roof.

She joyed in being able to sense its presence, the place and distance of it, the nature and character of its life. She could feel its heart beating and see through its feeble eyes. She was not content with just watching and seeing through it all. She reached deeper and made it move. She crawled it around in its little tunnels and then into the light. In its little eyes, the world was black and white, filled with bright and frightening light. It wanted to go down, but she wouldn't let it. She wanted to see the trees and rocks and grass. There was sky and hot sunlight. The little animal struggled in her control. It wanted to escape, return to the cold and comfortable darkness. It did not like the light.

Far above it, something passed across the sun, a confusing blur of presence. The poor thing tugged frantically. She wondered at its struggle, for she couldn't detect any danger in this blurring presence that moved above. She would not let her little animal go. She wanted to use it to see and explore the land above her.

Suddenly a shadow passed over her mind and the little thing she occupied was flooded with pain, and talons tore into her sides and ripped at her neck. For just a moment the ground fell away from her, then she tore free and pushed away all the pain and terrible agony of dying. She fell into her own body as into a dark well, and hid there, trembling.

Her reaction passed and she realized that the little animal was dead. She was not sorry, only angry that she had not sensed the danger or caught the mind of the bird. It had hurt her. She could still feel the pain of its talons.

She watched it soar away, arrogant in its dark protection. She wanted to use it, to see through its clear eyes all the ground it passed over, but she could not. It was like something else she had known once.

Then the bird was gone from her mind and something else was there. A sound. And in the direction of the sound—something black that frightened her. The sound grew to a frightening level. Dimly she could see two cones of light playing through the dust, moving in jerks back and forth across the floor of the cave. For minutes she watched, enthrawled, as the lights zigzagged closer and the darkness with them grew.

She could feel no danger from this, not in the sense that her master had feared. But the machine was getting very close and she dutifully warned him because she was in doubt.

Bork snapped to attention. His mind cleared of complicated thoughts and he concentrated on the present danger. He took one look at the machine, grabbed the native girl, and dragged her and himself clear of its path.

The machine moved by slowly, crushing the ring through which they had entered the mine. In the dim light Bork could see that a human form was driving the machine, but there was nothing to attack. Beyond a sense of presence and location, he could detect nothing but a shrouding darkness.

He instantly realized that this must be the human who had escaped from the mine. Bad luck—or was it good? The human was unaware that he and the girl were in the cave also. It could be captured or killed and the machine would certainly be useful.

With this in mind Bork moved rapidly to overtake the slow-moving machine.

Daniel was on the point of stopping the machine and resting when the left running light went out, followed closely by the right. A sharp whip-cracking sound accompanied each failure. Daniel recognized the sound. Only an air gun with explosive pellets made that distinctive swish-and-crack sound. Even as he was thinking this, a third shot came. It lanced into the foot-thick armor glass of the cab's window and gouged a small crater right in front of his face.

The flash of this explosion was enough to convince Daniel that someone was trying to kill him. He was out of the cab and down the machine's back before the fourth shot came. Safely behind the machine's great bulk, Daniel took time to catch his breath.

In darkness there was safety, and Daniel decided to abandon his machine. He dropped off and stood still, letting the machine draw away from him. He strained his senses to catch sight or sound of his attacker. It was sound that came to him first. Someone was moving ahead of and parallel to the machine. The sound of moving feet was almost masked by the noise of the machine.

There was the sound of another shot and a flash of explosion against the side of the machine. Whoever was firing still thought he was in the cab. Daniel followed the sound as shot after shot was sent in that direction. He was closer with each shot and soon he could see that there were two of them, vague shapes moving ahead of him.

The smaller of the two was unarmed. The larger had a shape and glistening skin that he recognized with revulsion. This one he would kill.

As Daniel sprinted forward the alien suddenly turned toward him and fired. The shot missed and Daniel ripped the weapon from its feeble grasp. He struck the gray-skinned thing sharply and would have paused to break its neck if the sound of his machine running aground hadn't stopped him. Its right tread was running up the wall of the cavern, and Daniel raced desperately to save it from turning turtle. He jumped up the side, pulling himself over the moving treads. The steel cleats and plates tore away most of his shirt and some of his skin. The machine was tipping steeply as he entered the cab. He grabbed and forced it into reverse. It stopped and began to back away.

When he returned to finish killing the alien, it was gone. There was no way he could find it in the darkness so he didn't try. It was more important to crush rings so no more of them could show up.

Bork nursed his pain in darkness. What he had witnessed was difficult to comprehend. After his first shot at the driver of the machine, the darkness that had surrounded most of that human expanded. Bork could still feel the man's presence, but he could no longer locate it. This had been terrible—to feel the presence but not to know where it was, only to know that it was getting closer and closer.

At the last moment he had glimpsed it and had tried to shoot, but it had knocked him to the ground and then disappeared again. But maddeningly he could still feel it alive and nearby, then coming closer again. He had run. Unashamed, he had run, having the foresight to send the girl into the darkness ahead of him so that they could both escape.

Now he rested and held his head. He felt terrible.

By the time Daniel came to the end of the ring line he was suffering acutely from thirst and to a lesser degree from hunger. Nearly two days had passed since the last meal in his cell. Activity and a constant awareness of danger had kept the demands of his body in the background. But now, with all the rings he could find gone, all he could think of was water.

His jury-rigged lighting was a poor substitute for the original system but it gave him enough light to see things within fifty feet of the machine. The walls of the cave were moist but this only tantalized him without satisfying his thirst. Try as he might, he couldn't find anything more than a bare trickle of dusty-tasting water, which he licked, trying to ignore the mud and slime.

He did find encouragement, though, in another way. While looking for water he discovered that a part of the cavern's curving wall was covered with a fine mat of tangled fiber. Examining these fibers in the light he found that they were tiny roots. And roots could only mean that he was close to the surface.

He gave this a great deal of thought. It was just possible he could use the machine to burrow his way out, even if the tunnel itself didn't lead to the surface.

He was too tired to start immediately so he tried to sleep, but he couldn't. Even when he put out all the machine's lights it wouldn't come. Instead he fell into a half-waking dream. His body shivered and jerked occasionally, symptoms of the withdrawal he was suffering from the yellow gas.

People moved in his dream. First was his father, who was crumbling soil between his fingers and trying to tell him something. But Daniel couldn't hear what he was trying to say. There was wind blowing leaves against a chain-link fence. Then this was gone and a big ship was landing on the other side of the fence. Daniel was waiting for one of the people on the ship, but as they came down the ramp, none of them had faces. The people stepped from the ramp and disappeared into the scorching hot ground. He tried to follow them, but the fence and leaves were in the way.

Waves were washing at his feet, and the fence crumbled away. Water buoyed him up and he felt that if he could sink he would find the other people. But someone grabbed his hair and pulled him up onto sharp rocks. He tried to struggle, but she wouldn't let him go. He tried to look at her face, but it changed and became gray. It was only then that he realized that his eyes were open.

The green light of the machine's panel shone on Derl's face. She was looking at him with a blank uncertainty, and behind her another face was staring at him.

"Don't move," she said, speaking without expression—distinctly like a ventriloquist's dummy. The red eyes of the alien watched him. In its hand it held the weapon.

"I can no longer afford to kill you," Derl said, but Daniel watched the alien. Daniel considered his position with respect to the weapon and decided that conversation was the proper course.

"What do you want?" he asked.

"I am glad you can understand me. Communication through this creature is an inconvenience and awkward, but her voice is the only way I can reach you."

Daniel looked at Derl's expressionless face as she spoke, and he felt a sinking sensation. But then he recovered. After all, hadn't he been a tool just like her only a few days ago? This calmed him and he began to think and plan. The alien needed him for something. He wouldn't be alive otherwise.

"If you co-operate," Derl's voice continued, "you will not be destroyed."

"Don't you have a voice of your own?" Daniel asked, curious if this was really true. He wanted to discover how dependent the alien was on Derl.

"You will be silent unless I bid you to speak. Start the machine."

The alien pushed Derl before him and entered the cab, but he was careful to keep her back, some distance away from Daniel.

Daniel noticed this fact, but pushed it out of his mind as he realized that what the alien really wanted was the machine. Daniel started the machine, then shut it down again as he realized the alien's situation. It must be trapped. All the rings were gone and the only way out of this underground world was with the machine.

"Why should I help?" Daniel asked, taking a great chance. "Don't you people know how to use your own machines? Does everything you do depend on slaves?"

The alien stared at him. Its eyes blazed brighter. For a moment it was tempted to kill him, but it could not do so without giving up. "You will co-operate, or you will die."

Daniel smiled at this repeated threat. It had wanted to kill him but it couldn't. The alien seemed to realize its mistake in threatening and it changed direction.

"I will kill this female human if you do not co-operate."

Daniel forced himself to continue smiling. "You can't talk to me and tell me what to do without her. So don't make idle threats."

Daniel's smile disappeared when Derl dropped to her knees. Real expression returned to her face for a brief second and then it was contorted with pain. She didn't make a sound and this made it worse.

"Stop it," Daniel said quickly. He started the machine as an indication of his surrender.

For a moment longer Bork poured on the pain, then he relaxed. He could not afford to really damage the girl, but he had to make the threat seem real. He was baffled by his inability to directly control the situation. Having to depend on voluntary co-operation was loathsome. He could never feel confident or comfortable without knowing this human's strength, and yet he could never know.

Daniel spoke and interrupted his thoughts. "If you want me to co-operate with you, then you will have to prove that I will survive the experience."

Inwardly Bork squirmed. He felt impotent in the use of words. He felt that they somehow changed the meaning of what he wanted to communicate. But he must somehow transmit power along this new medium and control the human. He sensed that his greatest chance to force co-operation lay in the use of the human female. Her memories showed a previous connection with this man, and he *had* reacted to her pain. Perhaps there was communication between them in some way he did not understand? Still, it did not seem enough. The man wanted something more.

"What form of assurance would you accept?" Bork asked through the girl.

"Discard your weapon," Daniel suggested. "Then we will both be disarmed."

"No."

"What would you suggest?" Daniel inquired.

"I am not the one demanding assurance," Bork replied, logically.

"Perhaps if you gave the weapon to the girl?" Daniel let the question hang. He had noticed that Derl's movements were sluggish, and if the alien gave her the weapon Daniel might find a way of taking it from her.

Bork thought it over. He had to do something to get the man to co-operate fully. The girl's physical reactions were not fast and her physical senses still seemed confused. These were bad, but he could still fall back on the threat of killing her if something went wrong. Bork felt that he must take this chance, so he agreed.

Daniel did not start working at the dig-out right away. He wanted to find a weak spot in the cavern's wall. The rock was coherent despite occasional roots and remarkably strong. It was so strong, in fact, that the only shorings in the mine were pillars of unmined rock at infrequent intervals. To dig through twenty feet of rock might take days. None of them could last much longer without water. And he was sure he could find another collapsed tunnel, and this time it would lead them to the surface.

He was right. The fan of rubble marking the tunnel's entrance was choked with roots. This was a good sign. The surface could not be far away.

Daniel started the machine's grinder and probed at the broken mass. It dissolved under the attack of the grinder and disappeared as rapidly as he pressed forward. Daniel glanced to his right and saw that the alien was watching him closely and that Derl, sitting between them, was faithfully pointing the pellet gun in his general direction.

The next few minutes would be crucial. Daniel also realized that they could be his last. Once they reached the surface he felt sure the alien wouldn't hesitate in killing.

Daniel threw the machine into rapid forward motion. He knew what to expect: the choking dust and rocks grinding against the window and pushing in through the doors. They wouldn't expect this and it would give him the chance he needed.

But it happened too fast. The dust and grinding rocks were there and then they were gone. The machine burst through the rubble and into the open. Blinding light crashed in on them. Daniel was blinded for a second. The glare was unbearable and his eyes watered as he squinted them desperately. The machine was still moving, canting to one side, and Daniel was unable to do more than fumble at the controls. He couldn't see! Not with so much light out there.

The machine twisted and lurched downhill. Daniel switched off the grinder and slammed the machine into reverse but it continued downhill, sliding sideways. The slope was covered with broken rock from the mine entrance, and the machine's giant treads couldn't get a grip on the stuff.

Daniel could hear Derl's voice shouting at him unhurriedly, and the alien was making unintelligible gestures, but they seemed little threat compared to this ride. The machine's vibrating mass seemed to transmit to him its own anger at the danger of this descent.

Forcing his eyes open, Daniel tried to straighten the machine on its course down the hill. He put one tread into forward hoping to twist it around. A huge shoulder of rock opposed him. The jar of hitting it ripped at his safety belt. Derl and the alien disappeared from sight, thrown out the open door.

Suddenly Daniel was looking down and nothing was between the machine and the upper branches of a huge tree but ten feet of rushing air.

Branches crashed and shattered with explosions of bark. The machine somersaulted and he felt sick to his stomach. Somehow it landed treads down and bounced. The terrible crushing weight of that bounce was the last thing that drove itself into Daniel's mind. The impact of it pushed him into unconsciousness.

Bork staggered to his feet. He was relatively undamaged, but he knew that something was dreadfully wrong with his human female. Her mind was a confused jumble of pain. When he discovered her body he understood why. One of her legs was bent at an impossible angle. She could move if he forced her to, but he realized that it would kill her if he did it for long.

Besides, there was something else that made him move away from her quickly. The broadcasts of her distress must be reaching far away because he felt the brushing contact of a group mind. They were sweeping through the area trying to discover the source of the broadcast.

As he scrambled away from the girl, Bork glanced down at the overturned machine. It would never move again. The machine itself was resting upside down, partially submerged in a small stream. Its remaining tread continued to turn slowly, clanking as unhinged plates passed over the drive wheels.

Closing his eyes to the scene, Bork cautiously tried to discover the direction of the searching group mind. He moved farther away from the girl. They would find her soon and she would lead them to him.

He turned his mind toward her and tried to penetrate quickly and reach her body functions, to shut her off. But he couldn't do it. He was buffeted about and could hardly reach to her emotions. Desperately he tried to impose calmness and caution, trying to get her to shut herself off. But he was only partially successful and he could no longer wait. The group mind was very close now. If he was going to escape he would have to move immediately.

This he did, but reluctantly. He hated to leave his tool behind, his only real chance of victory. But there was no choice.

He moved quickly in a direction that would take him back toward the central transmitting ring. Perhaps in the confusion caused by the native he could reach the ring and get a message off before he was discovered and killed.

PART THREE.

Awakening

Chapter 14.

Light, a cool breeze, sun's warmth, dry leaves, sharp rocks. These came into Derl's world of pain from the outside. She must make some decision. This was important, but it didn't come to her immediately exactly what she had to decide. She was dying. But the pain no longer seemed important. It was the question. Her body seemed to be waiting, hesitant and bashful. What did she want?

It seemed odd, and a smile touched her lips for a moment. Somehow it seemed to her that she had a great power to make a choice and everything else seemed to fall away before this power.

But this feeling passed quickly. Suddenly pain returned and it brought tears to her eyes; tears of pain and also tears of frustration and loss. All she wanted was to be alive. This didn't seem impossible to her and she was angry. Why couldn't she be alive?

The anger was very good, but it made her very tired. She needed to rest. Yes. She became determined. She would rest. When the tiredness was gone, then she would think of what to do.

Daniel woke to the sound of dripping water. He was wet. He opened his eyes. A knee dangled in front of his face. He lifted his hand and pushed at the knee, knowing it was his own but not feeling the touch. He was upside down, and shifting position slightly sent waves of pain from around his waist.

He fumbled with the safety belt and dropped awkwardly as it loosened. Blood surged into his legs and the puffy feeling left his head. He lay for a few minutes on the inside of the cab's roof, recovering. Then he pushed across the roof and slid into the mud outside.

The machine continued to clank away. Streams of mud and water dripped from the one moving tread and splattered down the steel sides. Daniel noticed this as he lapped at the dirty water dribbling from beneath the machine.

The source of all this water was a stream, blocked by the fall of the machine and now forming a small pond.

Daniel continued to crouch behind the machine even after his thirst was quenched. He scanned the broken slope of hill for any sign of hostility. The scraping path of the machine was clearly visible, and off to one side was a body. Derl. Blood clearly marked the jumble of rocks amid which she lay.

Daniel continued his visual search until he was satisfied the gray alien was nowhere to be seen, then he carefully climbed upward. He found Derl on her back. Blood was still running from a deep cut on her right shoulder and abrasions on both arms. Cloth had been ripped from her right shoulder, and a huge bruise ran from shoulder to elbow. But the worst was her left leg, broken just above the ankle.

He leaned closer and found that she was still breathing. Her eyes opened and she looked at him. For a moment he was lost in the exchange of glances. He could find neither fear nor command in her, only a kind of acceptance. He remembered the last day on the island and the way he had let himself fall into her hands. He'd done it out of exhaustion and necessity. There was a difference in what she was doing. Even without words he could understand this.

Her eyes closed again, with a hesitant flicker, as if she had been holding them open with great effort.

Daniel stood, slightly shaken. He looked down at the machine and stream below. Should he move her? There was no sign of the alien except a few footprints leaving the area, and Daniel could understand why it had abandoned its tool. He stared down at Derl for a long second. What attraction was there? It puzzled him.

He should leave now; merge into the wild freedom of this land. Instead, he picked her up and carefully began to carry her down the slope. She was light. He could feel the shape of ribs against his arm and hand. She must have been starved.

He reached a level place near the stream and laid her down. He set the broken leg firmly, glad that she was not conscious. He bound it tightly with strips of cloth and stiff twigs. As he finished, he caught a motion and found her eyes watching him. They closed immediately, but he felt a flash of suspicion that she had been awake to feel the pain of what he had been doing. He shook the suspicion away. She hadn't twitched or made a sound when he'd pulled and straightened her leg.

Lifting her again, he carried her beneath the broken pine and laid out a place to sleep for both of them. Low-hanging pine limbs hid them from sight and when he was sure she slept he fell into an uneasy rest himself.

Bork found the walking easy at first. He made straight for the main Nuuian complex, careful to keep his presence confined to the smallest space possible. So long as he kept himself close, the probing of the group mind was not likely to find him. They would find the girl far sooner and thus be distracted.

His path led straight up a small valley. But soon this valley became a steep canyon and then it curved away to the left. He could no longer follow it and get where he wanted to go. Instead he must climb.

Bork had always prided himself on his physical strength and his independence from instant ring transportation, but this was no short walk along level tunnels. He was already tiring with only a tenth of the distance behind him—and this might be the easiest tenth of his journey. He put all other considerations out of his mind and concentrated on keeping his legs in motion.

Trees towered around and above him. Each of them had a presence and character that seemed to challenge and disapprove of him. Tangled roots and brittle branches blocked his path, unresponsive to the powers he carried. He could see now why the Nuuians of the occupation force never ventured from the underground complex.

Bork shivered involuntarily. It was wrong to feel this way and he tried to shake the mood. The air was thin, the sunlight too bright. These must be what were making him dizzy. He was heartened to realize that there was a natural explanation for the way he felt. Doggedly he continued to climb.

The ground leveled suddenly. Bork stumbled into a clearing on the top of the ridge. The sun was setting in the far distance, but it was above the horizon long enough to reveal a tremendous chasm separating him from his goal. But at least the harsh light was gone.

Exactly what happened next was never clear to him. Maybe it was the oncoming darkness, his fatigue, or just plain carelessness. He hadn't seen any dangerous intent, or even detected its presence—probably because it didn't have such, or was able to hide them beyond his powers to detect. How could he know that such an insignificant creature was dangerous? If he had stepped a few inches to either side nothing would have happened, but his foot came down in the wrong place. He had stepped on it and the snake had bitten him.

He felt the pain and at the same time the snake came into existence for him. With all the power of his mind he gripped it and turned it to biting itself. The snake died quickly, but this was too late for him. In the unthinking use of his power he had attracted the attention of the probe. It was reaching out to him now, striking at his defenses, testing. The poison weakened him. As he withdrew farther and farther before the attack, he realized that they were not trying to kill him. They would wait until he was safely weakened and then they would come to claim him.

Daniel awoke in darkness. It was cold. Derl was curled up and sleeping. Daniel sat up and his mind was unnaturally clear. He could smell water, pine, many sharp and distinctive odors. He could hear wind in the trees above him and the steady rhythm of the machine still running. Everything seemed sharp, clear, and separate. He recognized this sharpness in his senses as a sign of acute hunger.

He went down to the forming pond and drank, then entered the cab of the machine and shut it down.

The quiet was complete for a second, then began to fill with smaller sounds.

Standing in the darkness by the mud-streaked monster, Daniel put his hand on the cold steel. He could understand a little of what some men felt toward metal. It was trustworthy. It responded with power and obeyed without question. But it was also cold.

Daniel stepped away and began to climb the slope of the hill. He followed the path that the machine had scraped in coming down. Starlight and a weak moon showed him the way. He found the entrance of the mine. It was blocked again with rubble. But there was something else he noticed that was more important. The trace of an old road could be seen leading away from the mine entrance and its tailings.

He followed this road as it wound along the face of the slope. In places there were patches of pavement, broken and split by roots and grass. But mostly, the road was covered by a layer of soil and fallen rock.

Quickening his pace, Daniel soon reached the shoulder of a ridge. The road curved out into the open, then disappeared again into trees farther on.

It was in the open stretch, on the crest of the ridge, that he got his first good look at the country. The sky was brighter in the east and it was no longer truly dark. It was what he saw in the valley that made him fall back into the shelter of the trees. A network of roads and buildings spread between two shoulders of mountain.

There were no lights, no movement, no sound. The city was dead, but he could not suppress the feeling that under it might lie a network of cells and rings and mindless slaves. The cold air made Daniel shiver and he retreated back down the road toward the mine.

The next several days Daniel spent fishing, gathering berries, nuts, roots, and anything else that might be edible. The things which could be eaten, he shared with Derl. The fish and other meat he cooked in the only way he could—on a hot spot in the machine's ore-intake throat. He had discovered the hot spot when looking for the machine's power source. Whatever drove the machine was sealed beyond his reach, but it gave off enough heat to cook, or boil water by.

All of this activity was just a diversion, though. Deep inside, Daniel Trevor was locked into the most confusing uncertainty of his life. He hated uncertainty and by the simple criteria of his whole prior existence there should have been none. He should free himself of this girl. She limited his freedom of movement. She crowded in on his space. He had killed before to protect these very things.

Strong as this impulse to freedom was, there was an equally strong push in the other direction. It was irrational. But the only way he could explain it to himself was that "listening" stopped him. Whenever he sat down and tried to resolve his doubts, he would "listen" and the future picture would always include the girl.

It bothered him. On the one hand, he resisted sharing the room he fought so hard to expand around him. On the other, he *wanted*. It wasn't sex. There was something universal, unexplained, and he glowered and paced and slept poorly. Then, turning uneasily in his rest, an answer came to him.

He was eight; a bitter and hard-working boy. Winter, with half an inch of snow on wind-blown, hard-frozen ground—and he'd just finished feeding pigs in the meager warmth of a shed. A scratching came at the door and in shot the starved form of a cat. And that cat had had the same thing in its eyes: Here I am. I'm *yours*, no matter what *you* want. Feed me or let me die.

And Daniel had fed the cat. Because it had been tough. Because he had "listened" and tasted a future with a cat in it. It hadn't worked. Cat had produced kittens. His father had discovered the hiding place and cat and kittens went into a bag under the ice. That was when Daniel learned that you had to make your own space and you defended it with everything in your guts or you were the same as dead.

He stared into the mountain air and then turned to where Derl was sleeping. He could barely see her shape in the darkness. What to do? He gritted his teeth in frustrated anger.

Derl turned slightly in her sleep. A frown creased her forehead. She twisted her neck, opening her eyes and staring straight into Daniel's. Once again those fears tried to overwhelm her. Just as on the island, there was something in the way he looked *at* her. His mind was a dark ball of chaos but a part of it was able to thump against her. Her breath squeezed away. There was a terrible attraction she had to this danger. Like a brilliant light—and she could no more retreat away than she could bring herself to feel safe in its radiance. She wanted to be close to Daniel. She had already made her decision. But she didn't want to be melted—she didn't want to become a camp dog—to crawl forward to warmth and strength and suffer blows and contempt in exchange for flickers of attention.

She closed her eyes and tried to gather courage in her own world of special vision. If she could somehow understand the danger. She reached out a hand to touch the blinding force that kept her back.

"What are you trying to do?" he asked in a cautious voice.

"I can almost touch—" but she stopped. She *could* touch. Her arm sank partway into the darkness surrounding him. She drew it back with a trembling struggle.

"What is it that you can see with your eyes closed?" Daniel asked with deceptive softness.

Derl opened her eyes. "You are almost not there," she said in a whisper, "but more *there*." She fell into silence, staring past him into the night. "They—they taught me to see. Much better than I could before. That is how they are strong and people are weak." But she could say no more about *him*. Is it total darkness that blinds, or the brightest of lights? She shook her head slightly.

Daniel shifted, sitting up. "Tell me more about *them*," he insisted. "Can you *see* them? Is this seeing you have—is it the way they controlled you before?"

Derl wrapped her arms around herself. She was almost more afraid of him now than she was of the Nuuians. They, at least, she could fight.

Daniel leaned closer.

"No!" She pushed him away. A wave of blindness washed over her for just a second and then she was free. She sat, numb, then slowly began to realize. For just the briefest moment her world had been totally black. But there had been no pain. And all the lights of animals and plants and distant Nuuians—they had all been gone. Was this how he saw? Nothing? Did it make him safe forever from being a slave? She sank back in tired thought, curled over into the warmth of her sleeping place and lost herself in strange dreams.

Daniel stood, looking down at her. Instead of anger at the way she had forgotten and ignored him, he was trying to visualize what it was like to discover a whole new world to see and live in. She was like a child—running frantically because there was so much new and strange to see in the world. He could hardly blame her for becoming distracted, or for being tired enough to fall asleep with words half spoken on her lips.

He walked away into the darkness. It was difficult for him to evaluate objectively when she was sleeping and snoring right next to him. He would walk along the mine road; take a look at the dead city. That would be a good reminder of what Derl's new world was really all about.

The cold was biting when he reached open ridge and he crawled into a jumble of upright rocks, warming them with the heat of his body. At least from here he could see the city, and the wind couldn't freeze him.

It was just a pattern of shadows on the valley floor. Not a single light. How many millions had *they* enslaved? How many millions had died working in mines? Daniel was puzzled. Everything he'd seen down there, with the exception of transfer rings, had been human-made. Didn't they do any work of their own? Or could they?

As he pondered these questions, something in the night sky caught his eye. A streak of light, dripping hot sparks. It dipped and swerved, coming toward him. It curved away at the last moment. The air shuddered and the ground shook with the impact. A bright flash lit the darkness.

No meteor, this, Daniel thought as he pressed himself deeper into his rock jumble. Air rushed out and rolled over him, then switched direction and sucked back toward the source of the explosion.

Chapter 15.

Robert Stassen had finally reached an agreement with the colony ship's captain. Stassen would be allowed three of the ship's smaller craft to investigate the new situation on Earth. But under no circumstances would the colony ship itself be moved closer to Earth than the moon's orbit. If he and the men he took with him did not return within sixty days, then the colony ship would depart without them.

Stassen's force consisted of twenty men, a shuttle-orbiter (which would be the base of the operation), and two small entry-and-return craft.

The shuttle-orbiter maintained stationary orbit above the area to be investigated. It concentrated on photo and radar study of the surface. The other two craft were assigned to a closer reconnaissance. Stassen hoped to get two men close enough to explore on foot without being detected.

As the ship plunged into the atmosphere it began to heat up rapidly. Lieutenant Greely glanced over his shoulder. "How's the altitude?" he asked.

"Eighty-four thousand feet relative," Harry Thompson answered.

"Air speed?"

"Three hundred fifty feet per second."

The lieutenant settled back into his seat and daubed at his lower lip with his handkerchief. It came away stained red. He could still feel the lingering ills of rapid deceleration. Just a few seconds ago it had been trying to rip the flesh from his bones. He grunted. Normally there would have been no need for such theatrics, but orders were orders. Stassen and the captain were scared, so Greely and Thompson's two-man ship was supposed to look like a meteor—but anyone with half a wit could tell that it wasn't. Meteors this small did not resist disintegration, nor did they reach terminal air speed before striking the ground.

APPROACH TARGET AREA UNDER METEORITIC SIMULATION No. 8. EJECT AT LOWEST POSSIBLE ALTITUDE. VEHICLE WILL SELF-DESTRUCT UPON IMPACT AS PER SIMULATION. OBSERVE FOR ONE WEEK ALL ACTIVITY IN OR AROUND TARGET AREA. SECURE OBJECT OF OBSERVATION IF IT IS SAFE TO DO SO. DO NOT TRANSMIT. ACT SEPARATELY. KEEP ALL ACTIVITIES AND OBSERVATIONS INDEPENDENT. ARRIVE AT RESPECTIVE RECOVERY POINTS NO LATER THAN THIRTY DAYS OF LANDING. IF OBSERVED ALPHA-ONE RECOVERY VEHICLE.

Those were the orders, simple and direct. Observe what you could, capture a living specimen if possible, and destroy your recovery vehicle if observed. Torching off his only way back—that was the part of his orders that made Greely uneasy.

"Forty thousand feet, twelve hundred feet per second," Thompson droned.

Deep in the pit of his stomach Greely could feel the last traces of weight slipping away as the vehicle reached a balance between friction and gravity. A meteor would have flown apart long ago. This was the part of the flight that made Greely uneasy. The seconds seemed endless and there was nothing to do but wait and worry. Thompson was lucky; as pilot of the craft his mind would be occupied right up to the moment of the drop.

"Twenty thousand feet," Thompson muttered, "five hundred feet per second and holding."

Only half a minute to go till the back panel popped away, allowing them to exit before the ship's final, fatal plunge into the earth. Greely reached out and touched the wall. In a few seconds it would give way.

"Sixteen thousand feet."

Greely craned his neck around. With the heat shield dropping away now he should be able to see the ground through the pilot's port. But it was pitch dark outside and all he could see was the back of Thompson's head.

"Twelve thousand feet," Thompson said. "Better check your chute."

Greely grinned at this advice. Thompson had a sort of graveyard humor. If there was anything wrong with his chute there was nothing he could do about it now. But he could check the straps securing him to the ejection seat, and this he did.

"See anything below?" Greely asked after a second of silence.

"Ten thousand feet. No, nothing—but . . . ugh."

Greely felt a sharp probing sensation in his forehead. He recoiled from it and shrank back down into his seat. "What was that?" he asked, shaken. "Thompson, did you feel something just a second ago?"

Thompson groaned and Greely sat back up and strained to see what was wrong. But he was facing the rear and there was no way he could get to Thompson without unstrapping. It was too late for that now. Too dangerous. The ejection would come any second now.

Greely had hardly finished this thought when he heard buckles snapping open.

"What the hell!" he yelled. "What are you doing up there, Thompson?"

There wasn't any answer and Greely ripped at his own straps. He turned and saw his friend slumped over the instrument panel. Thompson's whole body was shaking, except for one arm, which was hanging limp at his side. The limp arm began to move, fumbling with a holster flap. Thompson's arm finally got the pistol out and he twisted around, his whole body shaking. Greely couldn't believe it, but the pistol was coming up to aim at him and he launched himself. There was a shot. It stopped him in midflight, but he was close enough. He swung hard and knocked the gun away from Thompson. Then Greely saw his friend's face and the fight went out of him.

Thompson was crying like a baby, in misery, but his arm was still reaching out, trying to choke Greely to death. But the bullet's momentum carried Greely back toward the rear of the craft. Thompson fumbled for the gun again. He was about to shoot again when the rear wall blew away and Lieutenant Greely was sucked from sight.

Chapter 16.

It whispered and floated downward. Daniel looked up and saw it coming. He drew back against the rocks. There was something cold and dangerous in the silent whispering of the parachute as it descended. It passed overhead, its burden dangling, motionless. The burden struck the ground and dragged a few feet before the chute collapsed.

Daniel remained where he was, waiting. Nothing happened so he moved closer and could hear ragged and shallow breathing. The man who had come down on the chute was laying face down. Daniel turned him over and blood covered his hand where he touched the man's chest.

The moonlight was bright enough to make out features, and Daniel realized that the dying man was watching him with pleading eyes. There were tears running from the man's eyes and they weren't from the pain, but something more terrible. They were begging for some kind of relief from a torment that Daniel didn't understand.

The man spoke with a whisper of tremendous effort. "He killed me. He killed me."

Daniel didn't understand this, but he was drawn closer by the straining in the man's whole being. He recognized the uniform and the patches and insignia the man was wearing.

"He killed me," the man repeated in a voice unwilling to believe. "My friend killed me. Something made him kill me."

Suddenly Daniel had an insight into what this man must be and what must have happened to him on the way down in his ship. The man was dying, it made no matter what words Daniel said to him, but something prompted Daniel to comfort the dying mind and answer the question it was trying to ask.

"No," Daniel said, "it wasn't your friend who killed you. It was something else. I know what it was."

The man's eyes focused on Daniel and tried to reach out to him. It was the conviction of truth that the dying man felt in Daniel's words. His hand gripped Daniel's arm with sudden strength. He tried to speak. He wanted to say that he'd known all along that his friend really couldn't have killed him. His eyes tried to convey the message he was unable to whisper. The fingers relaxed on Daniel's arm, and the eyes closed.

Daniel stood up. He was shaken, not by the death, but by the tremendous gratitude that had pushed out at him with an almost physical force. He looked at the composed face. It was no longer strained by the horror of having been betrayed by a friend.

Derl woke and found herself wrapped in a silken cocoon. The sun was just beginning to peek over the horizon and shine through pine boughs at her. Her face was cold and each time she breathed, a puff of fog came out. She'd never felt such coldness around her, yet been so warm. The strange silky-black material was wrapped around and around her. She could hardly move and she wiggled and struggled to free her arms.

It was then that she saw Daniel. He was on a rock watching her. His eyes were blank, with a kind of coldness in them that she had seen once before—when she had come to help him and he'd almost shot her.

What was wrong? Why did he suddenly hate her? He was wearing strange clothes, and there was a dark stain on the front of his shirt. What did it all mean?

"Are you feeling better?" he asked, trying to keep his new feelings out of his voice.

Her eyes slowly kindled. She kicked angrily at the wrappings he had put around her in the night. "Why do you keep me alive—why do you keep me warm when you hate me?" She ripped at the parachute silk and forced her shoulders and arms out into the cold air.

Daniel felt the bite of her voice but he remained cold. He remembered the face of the man who had died in the night. Would he, himself, wake up some night with this girl's hands at his throat and something else looking out of her eyes? He kept this thought in the front of his mind and it made him immune to anything she might say or be. Because this in front of him was only the her of today. At any time she might become something different and deadly.

"I'm glad you are feeling well enough to move about," he stated coldly. He pointed at some food he had laid next to her.

She looked at the food, and the muscles in her arms tightened, and her hands made fists. She began to eat, but she didn't speak again and even when she looked in his direction, her eyes no longer saw him.

Daniel shrugged, impatient at himself, and walked away.

Derl looked at the discoloring bruises on her right arm and shoulder. They were much better. Her leg, also, was much better. But she could not push on it, even lightly, without great pain. The rags of her clothing would never keep her from freezing in this strange climate.

She pushed back the black silk and exposed her thin legs to the cold air and hot sun. Her anger was gone. In its place was a forming determination.

She must not allow herself to become dependent—not to the point where she hated herself and the one who supported her life. This was not what she had stayed alive for. She must gather her strength. Accept help, even, because she needed it—but never herself—she would never give up herself. She would *make* herself become strong—she would keep her eyes open, keep touching and learning about everything. She would *never* hide. Never again.

She breathed calm and pushed back her anger against Daniel. *He* was something she could learn from. She must understand what it was that made him safe and strong, even when he slept. She could no longer sleep as a child. All of that other world would not go away. The dancing lights of other life would play across her mind in the dark.

The Nuuians did not seek her, but they waited. She could see them, sitting in the distance, and she must learn a way to fight. And *that* was why she must stay close to Daniel. No more foolish feelings. She would have a *real* reason. In his stupid way, he was a protection. The darkness in his mind could reach out and enclose her also. And she would *use* him. One dangerous force to fight the other.

They both wanted to kill her, and she hated them. And she hated him more because it hurt.

Daniel paused to admire his handiwork. The grave of Lieutenant Greely was unmarked, almost impossible to distinguish from the surrounding forest floor.

Daniel wore the lieutenant's clothing and was grateful for the extra warmth and protection they gave him. The boots, tools, pistol, parachute, and cords—almost everything had been extremely valuable. It was possible now to think of something more than daily survival.

He walked back out of the forest and climbed to the clearing where the chutist had landed the night before. The old mine road was below him and the city, far down in the valley. The crumbling buildings and silent streets seemed to call him. The highway that followed the valley and curved into the plains beyond—once it had flowed with traffic.

Dead bones. Just like the lieutenant. Civilization had died here and its bones were indecently exposed, unburied. And as long as they remained so, nothing would grow in their place.

Daniel stood thinking. Wasn't this what Beta Colony was supposed to do—grow new flesh upon the bones? But Beta Colony was failing. Something else was needed. Something that would be resistant to the poison that had killed Earth in the first place.

Daniel returned to camp and he found that Derl had moved. She had crawled to the edge of the water, and then to the machine that blocked the stream. She had discovered the pack of equipment that Daniel had taken from the dead lieutenant and left next to the machine. Everything was spread on the ground in neat, curved rows, and Derl was staring at them with complete concentration.

She would touch something, turn it over gently, then touch something new. She looked up as Daniel approached. For just a second there was an excitement at seeing him, then her face closed. She watched him approach with neither expectation nor fear.

Daniel stopped, looking down at the display she had arranged for herself. At least nothing was visibly damaged. He silently began to replace everything in the pack and she continued to watch.

"I'm glad you are able to move," he said at last. "I'll cut you a stick for walking with, if you wish."

She looked at his face, then at her own hands and thin wrists, then back at his face again. Her lips trembled, as if she were trying, without speaking, to break some barrier that existed between them. "Why do you hate everything I try to do? I'll make my own walking stick!"

Daniel looked at her sharply. Not a whimper when he set her leg, and yet furious to the edge of tears because he'd put away some tools she couldn't hope to understand anyway.

"Look," he said, trying to be reasonable, "why don't we come to some kind of agreement? It's not *you* I hate and distrust. It's what you were, and what you might become again at any moment. It's something else looking out of your eyes. That's what I'd hate to see."

Derl looked at the ground for a long moment, then back at him. "Would you kill?" she asked.

"If I had to," he answered honestly.

Derl sighed. "That would be right," she agreed. "Kill it. If you ever see it in my eyes again, kill me. *I* won't let it happen again. *I* won't be alive if it does." Her voice had sunk to an almost inaudible whisper.

Daniel fell into silence.

"You think I am weak," she continued, "but my body is nothing. I can fight. I'm stronger than *you* think." Her voice turned bitter.

"You would actually fight them?" Daniel asked.

She stared at him with contempt.

Daniel ignored her, lost in his own thoughts. "Maybe we could," he muttered. "Maybe *we* could."

Chapter 17.

Sordin Raddi-Ka had studied the problem of Earth for the entire three hundred-odd years of his administration as occupation general. He still had not solved the basic and most upsetting of the population's peculiarities. This was the lack of what he had come to understand as a critical mass. Because of the extra resistance of the human mind structure, it was impossible to fuse the population into a workable and controllable mass. The whole structure of Nuuian civilization was based on the controlled use of critical mass, in their own society, and in the populations that they guided. He did not look at this normal relationship as parasitic. The fact that a small core of Nuuian telepaths controlled a large group of lesser telepaths was natural. The fact that the lesser peoples supplied their Nuuian masters with technical and physical comfort was also taken for granted. Should a body's brain feel regret because it gathered food from the efforts of a mouth and stomach?

It was the destiny of Nuuia to be the brain of the Universe, just as other peoples were destined to be the body. But humanity made a weakly body, one that rejected cohesion and threatened to disassociate at the slightest prod.

He had almost reached a solution in what he considered a supertelepath, something strong enough to simulate the Nuuian group mind and overcome the extra resistance of ordinary humans. But in doing this he had stripped the Earth's surface of usable telepaths. All that remained were extraresistant, except for those few who arrived every fifteen years to resupply Beta Colony.

Sordin looked upon Beta Colony, the ships that supplied it, and ultimately the worlds behind those ships as an inexhaustible pool to supply his experiments. And also his ultimate refuge and base of support if his conflict with the Nuuian Central Council came to an open clash too soon. They did not know of these worlds and would not be looking at them until the next hatching. This gave Sordin several hundred years to complete his work. In this time he hoped to achieve the impossible—to bridge the gap of space and time and connect the Nuuian Empire as it was ultimately destined to be connected—under the control and guidance of a single mind.

The Council considered this impossible, with good reason, and their belief was his greatest protection. But they did not know or understand the powers with which he was working. He fully understood why the most powerful minds of each hatching were dispatched to distant and unconquered worlds. He also understood why those that remained were neutered and made into inspectors general, or altered and converted into subservient group-mind controls. Only the weakling males were allowed to survive unchanged, wifeless, to serve the remaining stronglings, or to die if they resisted the limited but loyal co-operation demanded of them.

Sordin could see the wisdom of all this system, but it made sense only because mind control could not reach across the vast distances among the stars. Even the strongest and largest of group minds of the home world could just barely detect the presence of life minds on distant planets, and this only when the populations on those planets were huge. Only the home-world group minds had the strength to throw out the first contact ring that made invasion possible.

He hoped to change all this—to bring the whole Nuuian race together again as it had not been since the first outreaching. And once together, there was nothing to stop the next hatching being sent far beyond the boundary of this region of the Galaxy, or even beyond the Galaxy itself.

All of this was in the future, though, and depended on his success in solving more immediate problems. One of these was Bork Dakkett-O, the inspector general, and another was the escaped specimen upon which so many of his, Sordin's, other plans rested. He wanted to recover this specimen without destroying its usefulness, and he now understood that this would be difficult. One of his group minds had discovered the location of the specimen, but had reported a change in its attitude and susceptibility to control. The group mind had not effected a recapture because they had understood the importance of the specimen and its importance to him in a whole and undamaged condition.

There was also the problem of this new and unwelcome curiosity on the part of the space-borne humans. He had effectively dealt with their first probe, but already they were preparing another. He had no doubt as to his ability to deal with all of these probes, and even with the possible escape of information about Nuuians back to the humans' space worlds, but it was an irritation and bother on top of his other problems.

Sordin broke out of his long period of composed thought and rest. A human might mistake such for sleep, but a true telepath never slept. He might rest or become physically inactive, but he would never surrender himself into the helplessness into which humans continually fell.

He would act now with the true dispatch and ordered quickness of a composed mind.

Bork was still alive. This thought came to him as he surveyed his surroundings. He recognized the cage he was being confined in. It was of the type that restrained the mind as well as the body. There would be no escape short of death or submission. He suspected it would be the first of these. Why he was being kept alive he would soon find out, for the interface between the cell and the outside world was being activated.

The interface was designed to be a filter, resisting his power to the point where he could reach only a level of communication with those on the outside. So long as he was in the cage, and they on the outside, both parties would be safe from each other.

The texture of Sordin's mind appeared through the interface, and the interview began.

Sordin: Regret. "It pains me to confine you thus."

Bork: Neutral. "It pains me to be confined thus."

Sordin: Urgently. "Formalities must be cut short. It is important that you receive from me an accurate summary of the situation on this planet. Your freedom made this impossible before, just as your confinement makes it necessary now. The information you receive from me now will determine your future. You must recognize the importance of my ambition and subordinate your neutered power to my will, even though you may be stronger as an individual. If you cannot bring yourself to do this, then you must be destroyed."

Bork: Neutral. "I agree to receive your information."

With this settled, Sordin gave to Bork the outline and summary of the thoughts he had so carefully ordered in his time of composure.

Bork received the picture of unfolding years and problems and the untested potential of what Sordin proposed to do.

If Bork had known of the unlimited importance that Sordin placed on the native girl, then Bork would certainly have destroyed the creature and not simply abandoned it. But the past could not be undone and now he must consider his future. His loyalty to the Central Council, which had neutered him and granted him the extraordinary powers he possessed, was now being tested.

It suddenly flashed into his mind that the foundation of Sordin's plan was probably much greater than he had revealed—for how many other inspectors general had Sordin suborned? Were these others even now scattering across the Nuuian Empire waiting only for Sordin to perfect his star-gapping powers? Would their co-operation be the extra push that Sordin needed to win? Would he, Bork Dakkett-O, join himself to their number?

The breadth of Sordin's vision was almost impossible to resist. Was it truly the race's destiny to be united thus, through the agency of this alien force? Bork struggled with this question. Where did true loyalty lie? With the old order, or with the grand future of the race?

After long hours and prolonged composure, Bork came to his decision. Another inspector general would be added to the forces at Sordin's command.

Chapter 18.

Several times in the days that followed their truce, Derl tried to explain to Daniel what she had become, or rather, what everyone was, without being conscious of it. Even he, she tried to explain, was the same, but something in his nature was opaque, where it was translucent or completely transparent in others.

Daniel listened to the descriptions she gave of spheres within spheres and the way in which powers were different between individuals, how they diminished with distance. At first, he resisted understanding something he could never experience, but this changed abruptly. He began to form a picture of the future as he would try to shape it. It became doubly important for him to understand this world he would never see. He began carefully to memorize everything she said upon the subject of her nature and how it differed from her captors, the Nuuians, and how even animals and plants possessed differing amounts and natures she could see without the use of her eyes.

"Nuuian" was just a name she made up. In reality, she explained, Nuuians didn't have a name. They thought of themself in a picture, as the newest life—the foremost edge—the way of future time. It was difficult to put into words. She came closest by using her hands, clasped together in a small ball and then expanding outward. She also tried to explain the way "themself" was proper when they pictured their race. When they thought of themselves, the individuals, it was just a complex feeling of individual thatness. Just like *that* tree was one individual thing, or *that* bush.

Daniel began to feel some of the excitement she exhibited at the times she was trying to explain. He also wondered slightly at the way she completely abandoned herself and talked without reservation, revealing the deepest parts of her new experience. It was something he could never do and it reminded him of the basic gap that would forever separate them.

He would listen to her voice and realize that she was *too* open. She didn't have the same weave of impersonal, and yet personal, confidence and sureness that he had been building around himself all his life. She was attracted to new things regardless of the danger. She didn't have a sense of absolute rightness. She had no fixed sense of direction. How was it possible to live with such uncertainty?

Daniel would shake his head. It was difficult. He would strain occasionally and try to taste what it was like, but he was too cautious to abandon the firm ground he'd spent so long in building. Maybe it was fun to explore and look at everything with new eyes, but you *survived* by *knowing* where you were, how far you could reach, where you *wanted* to reach, and how strongly you could enforce your want.

He was content to survive. But he was mildly surprised that he began to look forward to dividing the food he gathered each day and sitting down to listen.

In her turn, Derl was losing the starved look she had acquired as a captive. She began to move about slowly on *her* walking stick. And she was becoming restless with the restrictions of camp life.

It was then when he decided to show her the city and find out if the fears he felt about it would be confirmed by what she could see.

It was close to noon and Derl was sweating with the exertion of climbing the steep slope from the stream to the mine road. She did not protest the pain that this climb caused her because some of Daniel's excitement at this joint venture had infected her. She was tired of confinement and inactivity.

The broken road wound through the forest and they walked side by side. Neither spoke.

Derl felt in her heart that Daniel was trying to believe in her strength. But try as he would, there remained doubt that would never be resolved until she was put to some test. Perhaps this afternoon would be an opportunity for her, or perhaps it would leave her broken.

This did not frighten her. She could not live without some confirmation of her own self-sufficiency. If she hadn't the strength to fight them, then she lived and was free only at their whim.

The road curved into the open, and the warm sunlight and heated ground were comforting. The city's desolation was not as pronounced during the brightest time of the day. Daniel sat at the edge of the road to look down at it, and Derl sat near him, but not too close.

To her the walls of the buildings and the shape of the landscape were just fleeting impressions. She was quickly aware that the array of enemies she had watched night after night lay in profusion beneath the soil of the city. They were no threat to her at this distance, and it was clearer to her—the patterns and order in which they existed. She studied this closely, her eyes drifting up beneath lowered lids as she forgot to use them.

Abruptly she was aware that they in their turn were watching her, just barely touching the edges of her presence. It was like a line of ropy light reaching out of the bowels of the earth and coming toward her. She drew back uncertainly, trying not to touch it.

She blinked her eyes open and tried to shake off the touching presence. She was unable to do this, but it seemed content to remain quiet, just barely touching against her—caressing her location and presence. It probed lightly at her character. She was unable to push it away. It did nothing more, though. Perhaps this was all it could do at this distance.

Derl touched Daniel and pointed at the foreground of the dead city. "It's there," she stated, "and there," as she pointed toward the highway leading out of the city. "There are two great clusters of light, powerful. One of them is touching me now. The rest are little lights, individuals, scattered on layers beneath the city. The clusters are deepest underground. One is always busy. It does something, sending things far away. It also makes the rings work when the other one can't. This is what frees the other one to touch me." She pointed again at the foreground of the city. "I'm not afraid of the individuals, but the clusters are strong, even at this distance. If we moved closer, they might kill me."

"Are you safe?" Daniel asked. "Can they move? Can they come after you?"

"No," Derl said and her face became puzzled as she studied the strange ropy arm that touched her. Its long, knobby length twitched and twisted all the way back to the cluster from which it came. Derl did not like it. The cluster itself looked like a cluster of fish eggs trying to squeeze together and become a big ball.

"No," she repeated, a trancelike quality in her voice. "Clusters can't move. They are different."

The words reassured Daniel, but not the way in which they were spoken. He could see that there was some struggle in Derl's face, but only she could judge what was safe and what wasn't.

"Should we move—get farther away from them?" he asked. He felt no driving need to challenge these things now. It would be better later when the girl was completely well, and when he himself understood more of what she was struggling against.

"No," Derl answered. She felt she was at a safe and comfortable distance now. She wanted to study them, watch them, while they were powerless to harm her.

Daniel remained silent and watched the flash of expressions on Derl's face as she resumed her concentration on the distant city. There was something eager in the way she looked, as if she could hardly restrain from jumping forward and coming to grips with her enemies now.

The eagerness drained from Derl's face as the ropy arm began to change. It was breaking into threads, and the threads were reaching out and wrapping themselves around and through her. She struggled, but they seemed sharp, like wire, and they cut deeper and reached for the part of her they wanted. She suddenly understood what they wanted. They were trying to hold her—to pull her closer—not fighting any of her strengths, but just holding her location and trying to pull it toward them. The threads burned her and weaved closer together as they got near their goal. They wouldn't let her fight. They just slipped away when she pushed at them, but there were so many and the ones she didn't push got tighter.

She struggled fitfully and knew that she must move. Her only hope was to move. She jerked and rolled toward Daniel. He was like a cold black stove to her, comfortable and solid. But the white threads shriveled back as if they were burned. They were helpless, burning away as she sank deeper into the cold heart of the stove.

Then they were gone and there was nothing but darkness and quiet and cold white ash.

Daniel watched, helpless, as Derl stiffened. Her eyelids fluttered and she fell backward into the dust of the road. Her body became limp, then twitched and rolled toward him, once. He reached out and drew her closer, not knowing what else to do.

She had said that more distance was safer, so he lifted her in his arms and began to run down the road, away from the city. He was so intent on moving rapidly and watching his feet to avoid a fall that he didn't notice when her breathing became regular and calm again. Her eyes blinked open. She felt dizzy, but she saw what he was doing: taking her farther away. Yes, she thought, distance. She felt drunk and weak from the power of her struggle. It was best if he felt that distance was what saved her, not the mere fact that he had been close to her. Everything around her was dark, quiet, safe.

Only the memory of the white threads reaching—pulling on her. It was like a bright spot on her brain. Her whole body shivered in a kind of uncontrollable relief. It continued to shake despite her conscious efforts to stop it.

Daniel halted immediately. He could feel the tremors that were rolling through her. He had a horrible thought that they were her last movements—that she was dying.

He looked at her and saw that it was something else. Her eyes were open and looking at him, embarrassed and ashamed. "I'm sorry," she whispered. "I lost, and now I can't stop—I can't even stop the shaking."

Her skin was cold and she was utterly exhausted. When he tried to lay her down as he reached the camp, she grabbed at him and wouldn't let go. He sat against a rock and held her in his lap until her head began to drop against his shoulder and she was on the verge of going to sleep.

"Is it safe?" he asked. "Are we far enough away, or should we move farther tonight?"

Her eyes moved beneath her closed eyelids. "It's safe here," she murmured. "I just need rest. So tired." Her body began to relax against him again.

He shook her gently, but she was totally asleep. He set her down and covered her with the thick volumes of parachute material. He sat next to her and decided that it wasn't safe for both of them to sleep at the same time. With this thought he layed the foundation of a fire and began a watch that would last through the night.

Chapter 19.

Sordin: Confusion. "What went wrong?"

Bork had watched the situation and as his was the strongest mind not directly involved in the operation it was his opinion that was desired. He had watched the group mind jell and coalesce under Sordin's control. Its contact with the girl-human had been strong even before the main effort had begun. Once coalesced, the drive to control location had been swift.

It was difficult, without the aid of a ring at both ends, to transmit or bring in a material body. There was too much chance of dissolution. But the group mind had been close enough and the subject strong enough to stand the strain.

In fact, the girl-human had almost been too strong. It had resisted the final penetration almost to the point of the group mind's exhaustion. Nevertheless, the capture point had almost been reached when the girl-human had simply disappeared, and the group mind's contact had been seared off with painful suddenness.

Bork considered the problem. He remembered the escaped human he had encountered in the cave. That person had been virtually nonexistent, all but presence and location masked by opaqueness. It was into such a being that the girl-human had disappeared.

Could this opaqueness somehow be shared between two? This was outside of Nuuian experience. But it must be accepted because it had happened.

Bork felt a sliding gap in his thoughts. To eliminate the opaque being, resort would have to be made to physical methods. But could physical methods be divorced from telepathy? Bork began to feel a swirling in his thoughts. He backed away from a dangerous chasm. To blank out the existence of telepathy and step into the blackness beyond—that was courting madness.

Gray sweat dripped from his body. He would have to explore the problem carefully before he tried to explain his thoughts to Sordin.

Sordin must comprehend the edges of madness without fully understanding.

Bork swept his mind carefully. He reached deep into the complex
to communicate with the biospecialist.

Biospecialist: Attention. "Yes, I witnessed partially what happened—mostly by reflection from the group mind."

Bork: Carefully. "Does what occurred have something to do with
the fourth structure of the human mind that you spoke of earlier?"

Biospecialist: "Most certainly. Language."

Bork: "Why hasn't Sordin communicated more on this subject to
me? Can it be separated from what we are trying to do with the girl-
human?"

Biospecialist: Hesitant. "I must confess doubt in my knowledge.
The concepts involved are difficult even for me to understand."

Bork: Insistent. "I must know as much as possible about the
qualities that make humans difficult to control and even—in the case
we must deal with—opaque."

The biospecialist composed his thoughts and tried to order them in
the best possible way. "I have broken language into three parts. The
first, which causes grayness and difficulty to control, I call names.
Names are what humans use instead of pictures. If I were to offer
you a goat (the form of a small gray goat appeared in Bork's mind;
the goat had matted hair, a small black spot under one horn, and its
nose dripped moisture), notice that you understand immediately
what I offer."

Bork: "Yes."

Biospecialist: "A human cannot do this. He must offer you [arbi-
trary symbol] GOAT."

A whole series of goat pictures flashed through Bork's mind as the
biospecialist illustrated. The goats grew and shrank, changed color,
horn length, facial expression. Bork was fascinated by the flashing
variety of goat.

Biospecialist: "I take these pictures from an actual human mind.
Whenever another human speaks [arbitrary symbol] GOAT, all of
these pictures flash through the human's mind. All the goats he has
ever seen *or* heard described! The result is [picture of faceless goat
with two horns in great detail]."

Bork: "Why are the horns in such detail when the rest of the goat
is blurred and generalized?"

Biospecialist: "A peculiarity of the human I chose for an example.

I assure you that all humans would produce a different [composite] GOAT."

Bork: Beginning comprehension. "Go on. Go on."

Biospecialist: "All reality is given [incomprehensible mass of arbitrary symbols] NAMES. Humans think in names, not in reality."

Bork: "This is what causes grayness, hardness to control!"

Biospecialist: "Yes. But let me explain briefly *why*. Absoluteness. [Picture of all features of best and perfect goat, alternated with all features of worst goat.] Some humans do not develop much absoluteness. But when they do, they become, in their own minds at least, the source and origin of the universe. The terrible truth is that there is some reality in their illusion. They do in fact become a source or focus of some power. Some become opaque, with a separateness almost impossible to penetrate. But in others there is the potential of an immense unifying power. It is by use of this undeveloped potential that Sordin plans to bring about the melding of our own scattered race into a single Nuuian whole."

Bork: Holding his head. "No more. No more."

Bork withdrew from his communication with the biospecialist and tried to absorb what he had learned. He dared go no further. The opaqueness of utter separation and aloneness—this, contrasted with the unknown potential of complete racial unity—it was too much. And there was yet more he had refused to accept in his communication.

Let there be peace, he ordered himself, swirling into the trance of slowtime. The aching in his mind grew less and he grappled, slowly, with a reality that was not reality.

Derl sat huddled near the ashes of the dead fire. Daniel had started it with a lighter from the parachute pack, but the fire was cold now. She kept the black silk wrapped around her.

Daniel was asleep and she just sat quietly and watched the distant activities in her mind. They were searching for her, but not vigorously. It almost seemed they were waiting, storing up energy for the time when conflict came again.

Derl shifted and looked at the stuff in which she was wrapped. In this cold weather she needed new clothes. She had been thinking of this for some time. It would take most of the chute, and a few lengths of the cord that Daniel had wrapped into a neat coil. It would take only an hour to make.

But first, she wanted to be clean. Only rain had washed her on the island; the salty water of the ocean was not good, and the spring water was too precious. Between rains, the sun and the dry, hot winds had been almost as good. But here the wind was cold and a rain would only soak the clothing you needed to keep warm.

She waited. The water of the pond looked dreadfully cold. When the sun began to warm the valley, she dropped the chute from around her shoulders and limped down to the edge of the water, using her walking stick. She hesitated, then touched the water with her toe. It was cold, but through the thick skin on the bottom of her feet it didn't seem so bad.

She quickly took off her ragged clothes and went in up to her ankle. She felt forward with her stick. The ground was slippery because it hadn't been underwater very long. When she reached knee deep, she began to hurry. The cold wanted to make her jump. Her walking stick wanted to float and she gave up trying to feel ahead. With the water above her waist, she began to rub and splash. The breeze made it even colder above water and she sank to her neck. Her skin prickled with cold and she moved, jerked, and rubbed quickly to keep warm. She dunked her hair and then she couldn't stand it anymore. She swam weakly to the machine and pile of rocks that Daniel had used to block the stream.

She climbed onto the rocks and then crawled slowly onto the upturned bottom of the machine. The smooth metal underside was warm with the direct sunlight. The warmth was almost an ecstasy of comfort, but the breeze against the water on her back made up for it. She turned over quickly, then again. The water on the metal made it turn cold and she crawled higher, onto dry steel. Most of the water had dripped away from her now and she collapsed on her stomach in almost perfect pleasure. Dribbles of cold water from her hair ran down her back and beneath her to remind her of how cold it had been. They made the pleasure greater. She lay still and couldn't move because it was so good.

Only a long time later did she slide back down to the rocks and limp back to camp.

The pattern she used was simple. Three long rectangles of material with a hole in the center for her head. She hung the three sheets, one after another, over her shoulders. They reached below her knees, both in front and in back. She tied the hanging sheets of material in four places on each side; a few inches under her arms, at the bottom of her ribs, just below her waist, and finally, about halfway between her knees and waist. She also used a length of cord to tighten the material around her narrow middle.

When she was finished she washed her old clothes and lay them on top of the mining machine to dry. She would wear these underneath and together the two sets of clothes would be much warmer than either one alone. She tied her hair in two rough braids, which just touched her shoulders on each side. Then she began to think about food.

She had watched Daniel fishing in the pond and this was something she could do without moving too much. There was a pole and line on the far side of the pond and she slowly limped in that direction, going toward the upstream edge of the water. She almost reached the stream flowing into the pond, then she stopped. Something had moved in the brush on the slope across from her. This was frightening, because at first she could see in her mind that nothing was there. Then she concentrated and looked harder. They looked like red-glowing coals—little, intense, burning with tiny sparks of hate.

She recoiled in her mind, then began searching in their direction with her eyes. The noise of movement came closer and she saw a bush moving. She held her walking stick in her hands and waited. A low, snarling sound came toward her. An ugly black nose pushed from the bush. Curled-back lips revealed white teeth and the dog stepped closer, then hesitated.

It had seen Daniel move and now it waited, uncertain of what to do. It wanted to attack the girl thing, but was confused because a real human was going to protect the girl thing. While it waited, a second dog emerged from the brush and began to circle toward Derl's right, upstream.

Daniel had been wakened by the dog's growl and now he stood watching. The two dogs were intent on Derl, but glanced at him occasionally and held back from the attack they wanted to make. Daniel held the lieutenant's pistol in his hand and he also hesitated. Both of the dogs wore thick leather collars that were studded with crude metal spikes.

"Don't shoot the dogs."

The voice spoke softly and came from behind Daniel. The accent was thick, but the words were understandable.

Daniel didn't move, or turn around. He kept his pistol aimed at the first dog, which was closer to Derl.

"I won't shoot if they keep back," Daniel replied.

"Why would you shoot at all?" the voice asked reasonably. "They won't bother you. They only attack weak ones, or slaves the snakes send out."

"Just keep them back," Daniel repeated.

The voice whistled sharply. The two dogs backed away reluctantly then turned and disappeared into the brush.

Daniel turned and faced the man who had whistled. Daniel got a quick impression of crudely knit clothing, thick beard, blue eyes, and pulled-down hat. Two work-darkened hands held a long rifle, which was aimed toward Daniel's midsection. Several other similar figures lurked farther back, obscured by brush and trees.

Daniel replaced the pistol in its holster. If these men were going to kill, they'd have already done it.

The bearded leader stepped closer. His dead-blue eyes held a cold and controlled curiosity. "Call yer girl back," he ordered Daniel.

Daniel didn't have to do this, because Derl began to limp back and came to stand by his side.

"What do you want?" Daniel asked. He was examining the bearded man as closely as the other was examining him.

"You escaped from the snakes?" The question was directed at Daniel, but as the man nodded toward the machine, it required no answer. "But what about her? You take her from them? Or did they let her go because of the leg?" The blue eyes held death. "Why don't you kill her? The dogs never smell 'em out wrong."

Derl watched. These men were like Daniel in some way, but different. She couldn't touch them. They were small, dark things, their presence just a bright spot hidden deep within them. They could not be touched. Somehow, because of the dogs, they knew that she was open and could be touched. Because of this, they wanted her to die.

Daniel could see this too, and he could also see from the bearded man's stare that there would be no relenting. For some reason they wanted him alive, but Derl was already dead in their eyes. There was no emotion in this. It was simply something that had to be done.

Daniel stepped forward a little. "If there is a reason she is alive, a reason why *I* want her alive, would you listen?" It was clear that the man's curiosity was the only thing holding back Derl's death, and Daniel was hoping to use this.

The man nodded, and Daniel stepped still closer. "Can we speak privately, where none can hear?" Daniel asked, and by the motion of his eyes, he indicated that Derl was the one he didn't want to over-hear.

The bearded man smiled faintly, clearly understanding such a need. He stepped back toward the machine and beckoned Daniel to follow him.

"You have some use for the girl?" he asked, intrigued, when they had reached a safe distance.

"Of course," Daniel replied, beginning to feel some small relief. "But first, tell me who you are and what you are doing here."

"Hunter," the man replied, not giving his real name. The crinkling of his eyes as he spoke made this falsehood mutually understood and acceptable. "We are looking for the metal that fell from the sky." He placed his hand on the bulk of the machine. "But perhaps we have found something better."

Hunter waited after he had finished speaking.

"Do you fight them—the Nuuians, or snakes, as you call them?"

Hunter shrugged. "What is there to fight? They stay under the ground, and we above. They used to send some like that one," nodding toward Derl, "but we kill them and now they don't send any more." Hunter paused and his eyes focused on Daniel with cold grimness. "The dogs find little use now, except to test the growing children."

Daniel looked at the long rifle Hunter held. It was clearly a muzzle loader, but was well made. Somewhere in these mountains a strug-gling bit of civilization was alive. And if it tested its own children in some horrible way, then it was keeping itself pure with a hardened heart. If it showed no mercy on itself, then it wasn't likely to show any toward strangers.

Daniel turned to look back at Derl, and Hunter followed his gaze. "Would you fight them if you could?" Daniel asked.

"Do eagles fight snakes," Hunter asked with bitterness, "when the snakes stay in their holes?"

"Yes," Daniel said, "but what if you could fight them in their own way? What if you had something—a sort of friendly snake, you might say—that would fight them, but wouldn't attack you?"

Hunter looked at the girl. She was looking back at him. If she understood that her life was in question, then she was showing no fear of the outcome. But courage like this was a minimum requirement in the world Hunter knew. He was trying to see something else in her face that he knew it was impossible for him to see. He had been on the slope in the morning and had watched as she bathed and made new clothes. He had hoped, as he had waited for the dogs and his men, that here might be a replacement for the wife he had lost, dying of grief after bearing and raising him three children who had not passed the test.

But this dream wasn't to be—just as no dreams but nightmares were meant to be in this world. Instead, he was being presented with an excuse to spare her for another man. He thought of this, but knew that it would not be his decision alone. The risk, or loss, she might represent to him was nothing compared to the chance that she could somehow fight the things he hated with everything of his soul.

"Very well," he decided, without mercy, "we will test how well she can fight them."

With this he returned to his men and explained what was to take place. They agreed, reluctantly, that there was no risk in what he proposed.

Chapter 20.

Derl stood at the edge of the brush and trees. In front of her was the highway and down its length she could see the rising structures of the city. Two of the bearded men stood beside her and she knew that there were others scattered on both sides of the road. They would watch and make sure that she died.

She was convinced of this, because she knew that she wasn't ready for what they were going to make her do. They were here to watch her fight the Nuuians and to make sure that the fight was fatal to her. She would walk down the road toward the city, and if she was strong enough, she would drive the Nuuians from beneath the ground and into the open where they could be killed. If she failed, as she knew she must, and they saw her falter and fall under the "snake's" control, then they would kill her. It was only with great reluctance that they restrained themselves from doing this immediately. They did not believe that there could be resistance—only that some people could not be controlled and that all others must be killed.

She had only one chance. She must somehow reach the protective walls of the city without being shot from behind or being seen and captured by the powerful group mind that was searching for her.

These bearded men had minds of a darkened and closed nature, not like Daniel's. They were very small and did not extend beyond themselves in the protection they offered. She could use them in only one way. They blocked sight, and if she kept one of them between herself and the searching group mind, she could hide in a limited way. But soon she would be stepping into the open and there would not be even this limited protection.

Daniel had been forced to remain at the camp, under guard, and she thought of this with regret. In this last night together, as they had talked, something had been different. The pulling and pushing between them had been gone. Perhaps it was only because they would not see each other again.

She had talked and he had listened, trying to form some comprehension of what it was like and what she would be facing. He had wanted to know about Nuuian group minds, their locations, functions, and the scattering and patterns of the other Nuuian minds. She had sensed some plan behind all his questions, but he had not told her.

She knew that there could be no help. She had answered his questions selfishly, taking comfort from the quietness of the spoken words. She had enjoyed it, just having the fighting barrier gone from between them for a little while.

Daniel had wanted to come, but the Hunter had refused. She was the weak one, and she would be sent into the city alone.

She looked at Hunter, and his face was hardened toward her. He nudged her with the barrel of his rifle, and she knew that it was time for her to begin.

Derl limped, with her walking stick, to the edge of the roadbank. All of her physical senses were very sharp in the cold morning light. She knew this was partly because she was trying to hide her other self, trying not to look and see all the powerful and blazing Nuuian minds that were so close to her now. Somehow, she hoped that if she didn't look and see them, they would not look and see her.

The climb to the road surface was difficult and she slipped once in the gravel and fell to her good knee. But she got to her feet again and made it to the top. Here she stepped into the road and began walking toward the city.

This was a different kind of road than the decaying one that led to the mine. It was covered with a glassy-smooth and transparent substance. She had to walk carefully and her bare feet helped her not to slip. There were smooth ridges rising from the glass and running the length of the road. These ridges rose about a foot above the road surface and they were rough on top, but as smooth as the road on their sloping sides. A big ridge, about three feet high, was in the center of the road. She studied all these things, and the cement and dirt and wires she could see underneath the glass, because it helped to concentrate her senses and blank out the certainty of her future.

As she walked forward, the broken walls of the city rose higher. They were old and crumbling, like the mine road. But the road she walked on was clean and unbroken. It must be as old, though, because there were drifts of blown dirt against some of the glass ridges, and grass and weeds were trying to grow there.

She stopped to touch one of the ridgetops, then moved again as she remembered that the bearded men would kill her if they thought she was turning back or losing control of herself.

The ridgetop had been cold and metal-like, not glassy like the rest of the road. She tried to concentrate on this difference, but it was no use. There were motions from between the buildings of the city and she knew that her time had come. Blank-faced people were shuffling toward her and at the same time she could feel the probing tests of the group mind with which she had fought before.

The shuffling people were in the open now and coming toward her. She raised her walking stick, trying to think of how she would fight them, but she needed her whole attention to struggle against the rising attack within her. She swayed unsteadily on her feet, then gave up trying to see with her eyes and fight with her body.

An almost physical charge passed through her as she sought to strike back with her only great strength. The shuffling people vanished from her mind and became instead soggy bags—filled with gray, unclear liquid. The bags were supported by thin lines of white light. And mixed in all of this were the threads and lumpy lengths of rope she had battled before. The threads were sinking into her, and the lumpy rope was twisting. She fought them and everywhere the threads curled back, but returned the moment she stopped pushing.

The gray bags plopped against her, trying to smother and distract her from the horrible white rope. She slashed at them with hopeless fury. The gray liquid bursting from their ruptured forms made her sick and she tried not to choke. There were more and more of them. No matter how many she burst they kept coming. The gray liquid rose in clouds around her, choking and burning. She felt a wrench deep within her and knew that the white threads had gripped her and that there was no way she could get them off. They pulled and tightened and drew her from all support and into a whirling of darkness and light.

She felt popping and breaking all around her and great rushing and pulling into soft darkness. Red pain and gripping pressure squashed down on her. She held on to the pain and bit into it. It screamed and tried to get away.

Only the blackness and pressure remained, trying to crush her. Then it tired. It drained away, coldly, leaving her in a world filled with gray.

Hunter and his men followed Derl as she walked toward the city. They never left the cover of the brush at the edge of the road.

Hunter watched as the weak ones emerged from the city and moved toward the girl. This was the first time he began to believe that the girl might have some strength to fight them—because, if the snakes must send weak ones to capture the girl physically, didn't this mean that they couldn't control her in other ways?

Hunter ordered his men into the trees. From higher up they could shoot with more accuracy down onto the road. As they climbed he noticed that the girl had staggered to a stop and that many of the weak ones had also fallen in a wide circle all around her. But still there were more, and they kept coming from the city and moving toward the weakening girl. He ordered his men to fire at the advancing weak ones.

Puffs of smoke and sharp reports answered his order. Weak ones fell, but if not killed, they continued to advance. The girl fell too, and Hunter felt a pang of regret that one of his men had mistaken his order and shot her too.

Then the weak ones were falling upon the girl and he realized that she must still be alive for them to do this. Then it seemed that they were intent only on burying her with their bodies and protecting her from the bullets of his men.

This thought drove him into a frenzy and he charged up onto the road. His men followed closely. They must make sure that this girl was dead.

He cast aside his discharged rifle and pulled a long blade from his belt. He and his men fell on the writhing mass of bodies and began to pull it apart, killing the unresisting weak ones. But when they reached the bottom, there was nothing there. The girl's body was gone.

A deep feeling of cold and the brightness of light seemed to coalesce around her. But Derl did not feel or see this. It was as if, for the moment, all communication was cut between herself and the outside world. She was aware that her legs were drawn up against her chest and that her head rested upon her knees. Her arms were flung tightly around her legs and held them close. She lay on her side, one of her tightly gripping arms being crushed, lightly, by her body.

But none of this mattered. A strange warmth seemed to fill her, spreading even to the tips of her toes. It was a very comfortable warmth. This was triumph.

In silent, unmoving stillness, she reveled in this warmth. It seemed nothing great, what she had done. She had not destroyed or created anything great or marvelous. It was almost as if nothing had happened. Only one thing. Something had tried to change her and she had not let it happen.

It had moved her, and brought her closer, and shaken her. But she was still the same. Now it was resting and this almost made her cry in happiness. She, all by herself, had made it need rest.

She was in its cage now, and it could come back to shake and tear and be mad at her. It could even kill her. But it could never make her change. She thrilled with this thought and knew it was a great strength inside her.

Slowly, other feelings came to her body and it began to breathe, relax, and sense the cold and hardness of the floor on which it rested. Derl stirred slightly. Her nose smelled metal. Bright light made her eyes blink when she tried to open them. She cried a little to make them see, so she could look at herself.

She slipped a hand beneath the black silk and felt the slow, strong pounding of her heart. Warmth came from within her to push away the cold feeling of her skin.

There was something new in the way she touched and looked at herself. She felt a strange sense of protectiveness. It was the first time she had looked at herself as something of value, something worth protecting. This was a beautiful secret.

She smiled, sinking back slowly and becoming asleep again. Traces of strength remained to make her sleeping face seem different than it had been before.

Chapter 21.

When do you place your future in another person's hands?

Daniel did not enjoy confronting this question. In his mind he had already begun to formulate what the future would be, when the power to shape it was taken from his hands. He saw no contradiction. He had already decided what his own *and* Derl's future would be.

But Hunter's arrival had forced a change and perhaps destruction of everything he wanted. Acceptance of this condition was the only course toward overcoming it.

He waited impatiently for the return of Hunter. He, Daniel, must know if Derl had survived.

It was close to noon when the first of Hunter's companions returned and spoke to those who had been left to guard Daniel. They would tell him nothing, but soon others came, and they were burdened with clothing and other material that Daniel recognized as the spoils of a battle. Hunter came last, with two of his men who were borne on stretchers.

When all were safely arrived a great fire was started and the cooking for a great feast began.

Daniel watched it all in a dark silence. Derl had not returned. Nor would any of the men speak with him.

Finally, a wizened old man sat by the fire and produced a stub of pencil and carefully unrolled several sheets of paper. Daniel edged closer and listened as speakers began to relate the day's happenings. The old man would listen and make a few notes. He was making a report.

Daniel shivered coldly. This was no band of random savages. Hunter was only a small leader. The report was for someone else.

Daniel thought of this as he listened. Derl's walk toward the city was described. The advance of weak ones and her fight with them. Her disappearance and probable capture were described. Finally the

chasing of the remaining weak ones back into the city where the
snakes had lain in ambush near a set of transfer rings. Here casual-
ties had been suffered and a retreat made. A careful listing of dead
and injured was made.

But Daniel no longer listened. Derl was still alive. She was probably underground again, in the laboratories and tunnels that she had
described to him.

He walked away from the fire and went toward the machine and
the edge of the pond. Hunter followed him and stopped him as they
reached the edge of the water.

"I am sorry I didn't fully believe you about the girl," Hunter said.
"If we had stayed closer to her, we might have been able to keep
them from taking her."

Daniel turned to face Hunter. "There is no way you can reach her,
where she is now?" he asked.

Hunter shook his head. "The city is a death trap. We can fight
them in the open, because the weak ones are slow and the snakes
don't see well and don't come out. They only fight where they have
rings."

Daniel accepted this. His second choice as a way to reach Derl
had been to go through the city. But if there was a physical connection between the city and the underground, it was too well guarded.
He would go the way he had originally planned. It was dangerous
but would forever free him of Hunter and his men. This was necessary. No matter what the man said, Daniel believed that these people
would kill Derl, in the end, no matter what value she might be to
them in the short run. It was too much a part of their life.

After Hunter returned to the fire, Daniel climbed the machine and
sat near the blades that had chewed into the mountain. There were
still several of Hunter's men watching him, but they had allowed him
to retain his weapon. Perhaps they were just testing to see how far he
could be trusted, but he was grateful for the advantage it gave him.

Casually, Daniel stepped among the cutting edges of the machine's
grinder and slipped down toward the central hole where the ground-
up coal had gone. He stepped below it, then entered the hole head
first. The bright sunlight was blacked out. He crawled forward toward the red glow where he had cooked fish for Derl. Beyond this
glow was a transfer ring. He was counting on this ring. It should take
him into the Nuuians' underground complex.

Derl had told him of the huge group mind that did nothing but send coal from this world to another. And this was close to where she would be.

He slipped past the glowing hot spot and crawled deeper into the darkness. The ring was just ahead, but he knew it before he reached it. It wasn't like other rings. It was designed to transfer coal, and this was almost a fatal difference. As he drew closer, he felt a detached sensation—as if his body were dropping away from him. His arms collapsed under him as he crawled, but his legs continued to push him forward toward the ring. Then they collapsed too and he slid the last few inches.

His head rested against the cold iron of the ring. It continued to struggle with him, trying to transfer the body, without the life that was attached to the body. This created a pulling sensation.

The body remained in the machine and began to turn cold. Daniel sensed this without knowing what was happening. The cold continued to spread and he realized that he had to stop resisting or the body would never be transferred. This was hard to do. He couldn't let himself be snatched apart.

He had no choice. He let go.

It was terrible, like a train swatting into him, carrying away his flesh, and leaving him behind. Then he felt a sucking wind, like the passing of something huge. He was pulled by this into blackness, then felt his feet jar into something solid and slide.

He bounced on a metal grid. Black coal showered on him from all sides, spewing from rings in the wall. It was heavy and pounded against him. The metal grid was slanted and it shook back and forth. He slid along it while much of the coal fell through into the blackness below. Some of the coal caught in the grid holes. A great blade scraped the bottom of the grid and cut through the clogging bits of coal. Daniel felt the high-pitched scratching of the blade as it passed beneath the grid he was sliding across.

He and large pieces of coal slid and rolled downward. A huge crunching sound came from ahead. Giant metal plates ground together and smashed the coal that hadn't fallen through the grid. Daniel clutched at the grid to stop his sliding. His fingers caught at the thick metal strands of the grid. He held on. The coal moving past him pushed and he slid around until his legs were pointed downward toward the crushing metal plates. He held his grip desperately until, suddenly, the high scratching noise came and he let go quickly. The blade almost snatched off his fingertips as it passed. He grabbed again to stop his downward sliding. The crunching of metal plates crushing coal was closer. Two- and three-foot chunks of the black rock bounced off his head and shoulders on their way toward destruction.

He rolled sideways, trying to escape the pounding, and slid farther toward the crunching sound. The blade passed under him again. He stood and ran, trying to reach the side of the sliding, shaking chute. The grid holes caught at his boots. His leg almost plunged into one of the holes. He became careful. The leg would be cut off if it was caught in one of those holes.

He reached the edge of the chute and gripped a railing, holding on with unthinking strength.

Minutes passed before his mind began to function. He watched, mesmerized, as the coal rumbled down to be crushed. There was a continuous grinding roar in his ears. He looked down, through the grid, into the darkness where coal rained down.

The railing shook and moved in rhythm with the shaking of the grid. He clung to the railing and crawled upward slowly. He reached the level of a platform that swung into and out of reach as the grid moved. He jumped to the platform.

Suddenly everything seemed tremendously quiet. The vibrations that had been shaking his body were gone. He lay down on the platform and covered his head with his arms. The darkness that swept over him was a bliss of silence.

Bork and Sordin stood outside the cell.

Sordin: Concerned. "She has changed since you were able to control her?"

Bork: Recovered and calm. "Grown more skilled, yes. I do not think there has been a basic change. It was I, personally, or the doctor, or yourself, who controlled the specimen. Not a group mind. If you or I were to attempt control individually, without going through a group mind, I think it would be possible. But the specimen is more skilled now, more dangerous."

Sordin: Agreement. "Yes. This is what I decided myself. Perhaps it is better. She will be of more use. I think, in fact, that I can complete an almost perfect union with her."

Bork was silent. Several times Sordin had used the personal visualization when referring to the human specimen. Was this just a usage that came from three hundred years of contact with the species? Bork did not think so. He had inspected many other planets, and no such possessive linkage had grown up among the occupation groups there. He, himself, had felt this attraction while in control of the female. Had Sordin, in his long contact here, changed? Was it possible to begin thinking of specimens on the same level as you thought of fellow Nuuians? As a part of the greater species?

Bork thought of this and of the great plan that had been conceived here. He was committed to this plan, just as he was now committed to aid Sordin in every way. But Bork wanted to understand the roots of what was happening. Success would depend on a full understanding.

Sordin broke the silence. "One of us will have to try. No others are powerful enough."

Bork: Seriously. "Yes."

Sordin: With decision. "It will have to be myself."

Bork: Understanding. "If you succeed, it will give you greater power and control, here and in the future. If you fail, I would have failed, and I will be left to cover, without feeling, the greatness of what you tried. I will mate with all your group minds, return our personnel and them to safety."

Bork did not need to elaborate on what would happen after he had returned all to safety. He was unable to fulfill a full mating with the group minds and after a time they would turn on him and kill him. But this would be a just reward for so great a failure.

Sordin: Anticipation. "What we do is a great chance. Nothing will be the same if I succeed. I will prepare."

Chapter 22.

Derl had moved to the far corner of the cell, as far from the door as she could go. Even this short distance would be of help when they came, because distance weakened strength, and they had the advantage of strength.

She was hungry and thirsty, because they had given her nothing to eat. She was tired, because they had tried to come in several times while she was sleeping.

Now she no longer tried to sleep and the hunger and thirst did not seem to hurt anymore. She was not afraid. Not even anxious. She felt calm, but was excited with herself. She was excited because she had a great confidence that nothing could break her calm. It was a strange excitement, this control of so great a thing as herself.

She tested the pattern and strengths of her cage with interest and care. There were places through which she could break and she wondered what it was that kept her from going through these places and turning corners. But she could only go straight, like light. Perhaps there were mirrors from which you could be reflected. She had never seen one.

She thought about Daniel, curious of the differences between their strengths. She wondered if there were some way, ever, she could be as close to him as she felt now to herself. What would that be like?

She took a deep breath and let it out slowly.

The door to her cell opened and Sordin stepped in. The door closed behind him.

It was like a great light filling the room, and the two of them seemed to touch and form a wall. The room was cramped but seemed to bulge as they both sought more space to fill, to wall off from the other. There was safety in space, and Derl thrilled in the knowledge that she had learned this from fighting.

Sordin was not in a hurry and because of this they remained separated by the length of the room. He did not try to come closer. Light sparkled and flickered across the surface of their contact. Sordin could feel the strength he was fighting and he hungered for it with an almost physical ache.

Derl, for once, was not defensive of herself and she tried to learn what Sordin was like. They knew everything of her so she must look in return and not hide. He was very strong and old. He let her learn some things, but worked to press her back, to reach into her beyond the point from which she could resist. It was a horrible thing he was trying to do. He wanted a shell—to drive out the living part of her, but to save the husk; to use her like a living coat, to hang her in a closet when the warmth and strength of her shell were no longer needed.

She felt a kind of sickness seeing all of this. There was no tolerance in her opponent for something outside of itself, something separate. And she was not only separate; apart from it, she also possessed power and strength that it wanted for itself. She realized, with a slow-turning revulsion, that it was almost like a cannibal, but it ate something that was more precious than flesh.

The room began to grow warm as they fought. Sweat began to spring from Derl's skin. Sordin showed no sign that the heat bothered him.

The wall and flickering lights between them began to dissolve as Sordin pushed more directly toward his goal of control. A single bright probe of red and purple light cut into her. She, in her turn, pushed in all directions—with great power, but without experience. She did not know how, or even want, to gain control of her attacker. If she could, she just wanted to push it away, to push it out of existence if there were no other place to push it.

Sordin was constrained against killing, but he knew what he was about. His whole being narrowed down into a single beam that grasped for the essence of victory. His flickering eyesight confirmed that he was striving directly toward the heart of the huddled form in the corner. It began to seem incredibly easy as he plunged forward through the writhing mass that now filled most of the room. She was conquering the space, but he was capturing the heart.

Derl could feel this happening too. She conquered the spaces of the room with the raging strength of a great empire. But at the core she could feel the pain of a sapping rot and weakness. Her strength was without use because it had no direction and he would not fight it.

She could feel the confidence in Sordin. Helplessly, she could see what he was doing, delicately cutting away the bonds that held her to what she was. It was a pain she could not stand. But he was used to the agony that burst out and filled the room.

For a moment Derl could do nothing but fight herself, and she gripped the shredding tears of agony—holding them back. She was losing. He was tearing her apart, greedily occupying the spaces that they could not share.

But Derl did not choose to lose, at least not this way, not the way Sordin wanted her to lose. All she had was strength. She could not learn to direct herself in so short a time. She had to make Sordin fight all of her, not just the part he wanted for his own.

Sordin felt the beginning of capture. He felt her giving way, trying to flee. *But there is no place to run!* he wanted to shout at her. He experienced merciless joy. Then Derl's body jerked and moved. Sordin exulted at this final weak effort to escape. The beam of his power swung to follow, tearing through the sweep of space that she controlled. The girl's body shuddered as he fixed on it the shaft of his focused power. He quelled its power to move.

Again he tried to make the final capture, but she moved again, only this time it was with a horrible swiftness. Her body slumped into laxness, abandoned. Sordin found himself sweeping through the space of the room, like a searchlight sweeping through thick fog, back and forth, frantically seeking the essence he had so nearly severed and destroyed. But the dark fog of the room was filled with her power and strength and it shredded and tore at the brilliance of his searchlight. He weakened, desperately trying to pin down the elusive flight. At last, in panicked effort, he tried to switch to defense, to reassemble the wall, but what he had left was so small that it was pushed from his body and through the fine mesh of the cage and into the nonending space beyond.

Sordin's body remained undisturbed. For a few moments it continued to function as a complicated chemical machine. Then it stopped and remained still.

Sordin was dead. Bork felt no anger or need for revenge because of this. It was simply the alternative to victory and a greater future for the Nuuian race. Now survival was the concern of the race, and Sordin had assigned Bork the responsibility for this.

He mated with the group minds that had been Sordin's and began to dismantle the Nuuian presence on Earth. There were eighteen mining operations scattered across the planet, and the first thing he did was to discontinue the homeward transfer of coal. The undeveloped egg hatches were collected and transmitted to safety. Following these, all the outlying personnel were collected and sent after them. This left only the central control complex to evacuate.

Bork did not open the door to the cell in which Sordin had died. This was too dangerous. But he was concerned about the body. It was evidence that he did not care to leave behind. Was there a chance of it being discovered in the near future? Not if he took the proper precautions. The two tunnels leading up into the city had long been sealed. This left the human workers in the cell complex. After the last Nuuian had departed, they might break out and somehow reach the surface.

There was an easy solution to this. Bork simply had them transported through the rings into the dead city. Here they would be allowed to go free of control. They would soon be killed by their own people or wander away, having no real memory of their captors.

When Bork had finished this, he gathered all secondary personnel and had them transmitted homeward. He alone remained on Earth with the two group minds with which he had mated. Even though these group minds would eventually kill him, he had to save them. They were too valuable and too illustrative to leave behind. The first was no problem. It could be sent by the other. But how would he and the final group mind escape?

The solution was taken out of his hands. Alerted by the refugees sent before him, the powerful group minds of the Central Council reached out and assisted in his evacuation. Nothing was left behind but Sordin's body, numerous meaningless metal rings, and eighteen tunnel and mining complexes. There were no records, pictures, or writings of any kind, because Nuuians had no writing or language that could be recorded on paper. All of the machinery, rings, tunnels, etc., were of human construction. Nuuians did not make or build anything. They used.

When the next hatching came, there would be one small area of the galaxy to avoid.

Chapter 23.

At first Daniel thought he was deaf. He could hear nothing. Then he sat up and heard the rustle of his clothing and the sound of his boots against the metal of the platform. Coal was spread on the slanting chute next to him, but the coal was no longer moving.

Daniel stood and hurried down the length of the platform. He could think only that this silence meant that he had been detected in some way.

He reached stairs leading down into darkness. He hesitated. Glancing up, he saw that there was a tunnel slanting up through the rock above him. This tunnel was bare and had an abandoned look. He climbed over the platform railing, scrambled across a bare stretch of rock, and entered the abandoned tunnel. This climbed steadily and he followed it as fast as he could move. There was no lighting and soon he could see only a few feet ahead.

The tunnel turned, curving to a right angle from its former course, still angling upward steeply. He followed the curve, and the darkness became complete. The upward angle of the tunnel was about fifteen degrees and he calculated that he was climbing about one foot for every six feet he went forward. The tunnel was about twenty feet high, the same width, with a squarish shape and rounded corners. It was probably the work of a machine like the one he had been using in the coal mine.

The tunnel turned again and Daniel felt along the wall to keep from falling or running into things. After yet another turn, Daniel realized that the tunnel was ascending in a broken, squared-off spiral. There was light ahead now and Daniel slowed down. He drew his pistol and entered a leveled-off space. The tunnel branched. A rough, unfinished tunnel continued to climb. A leveled, lighted section of tunnel broke away to his left. It ran a hundred yards and ended in a plug of concrete and stone. Daniel pounded on this in several places and determined that it was both thick and solid. Whatever lay beyond the plug was out of his reach.

He returned to the rough tunnel again and climbed until he reached the next lighted and leveled branching. This one was not blocked off and Daniel held back in the shadows, studying it.

The tunnel seemed to stretch ahead for miles. It was brightly lit, and there were rings and doors at regular intervals along its length. But there was no movement, and no sound. Daniel reached the first door and pushed it open. A laboratory. There were bits of bone on a countertop, flasks, liquids, a container filled with boiling water. Daniel looked at the boiling water. It was almost gone. The container's sides were stained with dried residue.

Everything looked completely abandoned.

Daniel paused to think. He could not search this entire level for Derl. It would take days. He reconstructed in his mind the description she had given him of the cage where she had been kept during her first imprisonment. It was higher, closer to the surface of the ground.

He re-entered the rough tunnel and began to climb again. Twice he passed closed-off tunnels filled with cement. Finally he reached another long corridor. This was similar to the first, except that the rings in the floor and the doors were more widely spaced.

Here he began to search.

It was the glow that first attracted him. The outer room was in darkness, but a glow was coming through the small window of a second door.

There was a drop bar and a dead bolt fastening the door, but no lock. Daniel threw these open hurriedly and pushed on the door. At first it didn't move, and he peered inside as he continued to push. He could see in the dim, glowing light that Derl lay sprawled on the floor. He pushed the door inward with a jerk. A puff of air escaped, almost as if there had been a pressure holding the door tight. As he entered, the door swung shut behind him, slowly, then with a swift sucking sound.

He knelt beside Derl and put an arm beneath her back and began to lift, but he stopped when he felt the terrible lightness. She felt almost weightless and he knew that feeling—it came from being on the border between life and death. For a moment the sensation kept him frozen. Her back rested on his arm, partially lifted, and her head was turned sideways, flung back and resting on the ground. He couldn't seem to move. Instead he watched her, his whole concentration fastened upon the instant of time.

She seemed very beautiful to him in that instant. His free hand moved and he placed it on the curve of her neck, gently, almost without touching her. Her skin was cold. A faint murmur of pulse touched him through the cool skin.

He continued to hold her, motionless, afraid that at the slightest slip she would leave. Only his eyes could move and they followed the line of her jaw and the curves of her face. He could not feel love or sadness. It was very important only to be honest. He wanted her to live. He admired the strength that was relaxed now and less asserted in her face. He thought, almost, that she was listening. This is why he did not pretend or feel anything that wasn't real. But I do want you to live. He could feel this, and say it.

The brightness in the room seemed to dim. Daniel felt a contraction in Derl's throat and she swallowed. Her weight seemed to come back to her and it was real against his arm. He lowered her gently down. She coughed weakly, once, then her eyes flickered, but remained closed. She smiled secretly, then frowned in puzzlement. Her dry tongue touched and moved against her lips. The lips were dry too.

Suddenly the room seemed very normal, and Daniel wiped the moisture from his hands. He felt a little unsteady, lightheaded. A weakness washed through him and he shook his head. He tried to recover composure by looking around at the rest of the room.

It was very ordinary, bare, dimly lit. A gray-skinned Nuuian was seated comfortably against the wall next to the door, asleep. This brought Daniel to his feet. He stepped toward the figure, his weapon ready. He touched the forehead with the gun barrel. Nothing. He pushed it back, lifting the head. The Nuuian's eyes were open. Daniel flinched back at the sight of them, letting the head fall forward again.

The eyes. Daniel remembered the first time he'd seen Nuuian eyes —and they had been warm, intense velvet-red. This dead Nuuian had flattened, blue-black eyes—sunken, like fresh bruises. Daniel stepped back, surveying the body to see if there were any mark or wound. Nothing, just the eyes.

No longer wishing to tarry, Daniel returned to Derl and lifted her in his arms. When he reached the door, it was closed. He kicked it and it rebounded open a few inches. He thrust his foot into the opening and swung the door wide. He went through the darkened outer room and into the corridor beyond. Only when he was a good distance away did he stop, lower Derl to the ground, and begin to give her small amounts of water from the canteen he carried.

She licked at these and swallowed. Daniel continued to give her water and he waited.

In the six hours since Daniel had given the last of his water and food to Derl, they had explored most of the upper two levels of the Nuuian complex. There was no way out. Both of the spiral tunnels were plugged with vast amounts of concrete. There were numerous air shafts, but these were too small to provide an escape.

Derl limped behind Daniel and did not utter any complaints. She waited in the main corridor while he explored rooms and interconnecting smaller tunnels that always led nowhere. The vast emptiness of the complex was new to her. Everything was gone. There were no Nuuians, or even their slave humans. The Nuuians had fled, and Derl knew that there was good reason behind their flight.

She remembered her fight with Sordin quite clearly. It was strange that she felt no elation at her victory. Perhaps this was because she had come to know Sordin very well in the few moments when he had almost been the victor. She could see back on this time and study it now. Sordin had fought her knowing that he might lose. Perhaps he had even wanted to lose.

No. Sordin had not wanted to lose. He had wanted to win and use her to wield his race into something greater. She had fought him. She knew how much he had wanted to win. But there had been something else in his mind. He had been afraid. The changes he had wanted to bring—they led into the unknown. He was reassured in his fighting that by losing he could leave his race and the Nuuian worlds in the safety of the past. His death would cause the breaking of contact between the two races.

Sordin had thus fought with the sureness of victory in any outcome, because the fight itself would resolve the dilemma of a slave race that could not be completely conquered.

Derl licked her lips as she thought of these things. There was something important in Sordin's fears that she wanted to understand. Something of Sordin's strange admiration for herself had touched her. In those last seconds of their fight Sordin had not wanted to die. He had wanted to become *her* slave. This made Derl tremble inside.

If she had known, if she had not killed him so quickly, would she have taken him and accepted his body as her tool. She felt sick when she thought of this.

The certainty of being slave or master. This is what made life possible for a Nuuian. There was no uncertainty in Nuuian life.

Derl did not know. She was uncertain many times.

She looked at Daniel. Was there some answer in him? He always seemed to know exactly what he wanted to do. But at the same time, it was clear that he couldn't be a master or a slave—not in the complete sense that she had glimpsed. Not with the willing, almost greedy acceptance that Sordin had tried to give her in those last moments.

Daniel sat down next to her with a heavy sigh. "We are trapped," he said, "unless there is some way you can make the rings work." He looked at her with mixed hope and tiredness.

"No." She shook her head. "The rings will never work again—not in the way they worked before. They are like leaves that have fallen from a dead tree."

Daniel leaned his head back against the wall. He laughed with bitter irony. "I never expected that they would run away."

Derl leaned her head on his shoulder. She was tired. Somehow she guessed that he had wanted to fight and destroy them with his own hands. He felt cheated because they had given up and gone away.

Daniel watched as she leaned against him and then as she fell into sleep almost instantly. Her breathing became regular. She was content in her sleep. Daniel felt trapped by this contentment. She should care more about the future that faced them. But he did not move or do anything that might disturb her sleep. Soon he was sleeping himself.

Chapter 24.

The broad plain at the base of the mountains seemed to be a perfect place to land. The shuttle craft descended with the haste of a vehicle that is only marginally designed for flying.

Ever since viewing the films that had come back from the first unsuccessful landing try, Stassen had realized that he would have to go down himself. But first there were precautions to be taken.

The colony ship had departed from the moon and had gone toward Saturn to collect fuel. When Stassen had ordered that, only he and the captain knew that the colony ship would not be coming back to Earth. This had been a prearranged precaution on their parts. Whatever had made Thompson shoot Lieutenant Greely, it could act at a distance, and Stassen wanted the colony ship to put so much distance between itself and Earth that there would be no danger. It, at least, must reach home and report what had happened.

He and the eighteen other men with him were on Earth for good, even though *they* did not know it yet. If everything went well, they would survive and the next colony ship would pick them up and take them back. That would be in fifteen years. By then, they might not want to go back.

He stopped thinking of this and concentrated on the landscape outside. The shuttle had landed within half a mile of the road that led into the town. Stassen and ten of the men with him got out of the ship and walked toward the road. The others remained to guard the shuttle. It was their only source of power, and more important to Stassen, it was transmitting everything that happened back to the colony ship so that there would be more evidence—more knowledge to take home.

The road continued without a break into the town and as they approached the buildings a bloody spectacle was spread before them. There were perhaps fifty bodies in the road. All of them were stripped of clothing.

What interested Stassen as he inspected several was the lack of any expression on their faces. Usually when you died violently, there was some evidence of the pain left in your expression. But the blankness in all of these reminded Stassen of what he had seen in Thompson's face as he had killed Greely.

They left the bodies behind and entered the city. The men were quiet as they searched, partly because they didn't exactly understand what they were searching for, and partly because they were scared and didn't want to reveal the fact to themselves.

It was Corpsman Ellis who found the tunnel. At first he thought it was a pit. Brush and a fallen tree partly covered the opening. But something made him work for fifteen minutes clearing the tunnel opening. When he finished this, he wandered off to report what he had found.

"Why didn't you use your radio to report the find the minute you found it?" Stassen demanded.

Ellis's face was blank. "Radio?" For a minute it seemed that he had forgotten what a radio was. Then his face cleared. "I—I guess I must have been excited?" He didn't sound sure.

Stassen grunted, but he asked no more questions. He resolved, however, that Ellis would never be allowed to get behind him or work alone again. The other men had also seen the film of Thompson and Greely, and they too began to watch Ellis with unusual care. But Ellis seemed to have returned to normal and the blankness did not return to his face.

The first explosion barely shook the ground, but it was enough to wake Daniel. He looked around him, startled. Derl was gone. As he stood up, he saw that she had gone into one of the laboratories, and he followed. Her back was to him and she was leaning on a shelf, looking into a mirror. She was smiling, looking at herself in a wondering way, and when she saw him, she smiled more and laughed.

He smiled back, involuntarily, unable to understand.

She rolled against the shelf, turning to face him. Then she stood up straighter. "You're awake!" she said. She tried to make herself look more serious.

"Yes?" Daniel said. He sat down, still puzzled.

She limped toward him with a kind of hopping gait, like someone with a nail in one foot.

Daniel reached out, thinking she was going to fall, but instead she jumped and landed against him, almost knocking him over backward. She curled herself in his lap and lay her head against his chest and shoulder. Almost incredibly, she began going to sleep.

Another explosion shook the floor slightly.

"Don't move," Derl said. She sounded tired, serious, no longer laughing or sleeping. "What is it like where you come from? Where people can fly in the air and do other things?"

Daniel listened closely. Her question was spoken so seriously that he knew the shortest route to an explanation for the explosions lay in answering.

"It's like here, only with bigger cities and with living people in the cities."

She pushed back and looked into his eyes. "Why did you come? Why did you come from the ship? Because you killed people?"

Daniel looked at her, wondering how she knew that. None of the other colonists had known—only Stassen. "Partly," Daniel answered, "partly because of that—and partly because I wanted to come. I wanted to live."

"And now?" she asked, her eyes round and watching. "Why did you come after me? I would be dead if you hadn't come." She spoke, almost challenging, but almost afraid—her eyes searching his face and listening for some answer they could never see.

He realized at once that he must be careful and that what happened in the future might depend on how he resolved this. Almost as he thought this and tried to formulate a careful answer, he saw her expression cloud over. She looked away and got down from his lap and stood, bracing herself with one arm against the chair.

"Why didn't you leave me to die?" she asked. She was looking at him now with an indeterminate expression, a mixture of pain and almost hatred. "I can't understand! You can't just answer. You have to plan and think; and you look at me as if I were something—something that wasn't alive!"

Daniel stirred under this. He reached out and took Derl by both shoulders and he held her at arm's length. "Look at me!" he said, demanding. And she did, not complaining of the pain his grip was causing. "You've asked me before—this question, 'Why?' 'Why?' 'Why?' Do you really want to know? No. You want me to lie to you, to say and do things you want, but that really are not there.

"You're something special to me. You are something special to all of us, to our world, our history even. Some would kill you because of it. I almost did. But now I save you, and I do my best to keep you alive.

"And it's not because I love you, or anything like that. It is because I want to know about you—know about the world you've seen here, which I can't see, which no one is ever going to see again. You can know what is in some men's minds. You know how they can be made into slaves and how they can be safe. I want to save all this—to make what you know into knowledge that will keep it from happening again. I will do everything in my power to learn and to make you stay with me until I know it all.

"This is why. It is also why I will not pretend or lie to you. I want all the truth of what you know, so truth is all I will give *you*. It is something we can't steal from each other. Maybe you will give it back to me. Maybe you already are."

He let go of her and she stood back a few steps, trembling. Her eyes were widened, as if she confronted something not human, monstrous. "You can't do it. Nothing can force me. I am so great, so valuable, but you want to put me in a cage—just like they did."

Daniel looked down, not wanting her hate, but he looked up again to show his resolution. "I would rather force you, than lie to you. I would rather be enemies and know you."

"Yes, we can be enemies," Derl said. She could not say anything more and she turned away, limping to the door.

Daniel stood and followed slowly.

A third explosion shook the ground. It was closer and louder than the others. Derl turned in the doorway and faced Daniel, holding the wall for support. "I—I made them come," she said. "They are people from your world. They are saving us, blowing up the cement in the tunnels." Her eyes wavered and could no longer meet his. "It was why I was so happy. I thought I could do something for us—for you—to pay back—" She stopped. She looked up at him again. "But now we have to fight and see who will win with force. Two monsters—"

Daniel struck her, but he held back so much on the blow that it failed in its purpose and she remained conscious. She slid backward along the wall and fell to the ground. She did not try to get up or fight back when he knelt and put his hand over her mouth and nose. But she began to cry and tried to look away from him.

"I'm sorry," he said as she struggled involuntarily for breath. "But I can't fight you fairly, I can't trust that you don't really mean it. You're too valuable. I can't let you kill me yet."

When she was unconscious, he let her breathe again and lifted her from the ground. He moved down the corridor, toward the tunnel the explosions were coming from. When he reached the end, he entered the darkness and went down the rough-cut tunnel toward the next corridor below. He stopped, however, and waited at the first of the turns. From there he could see light from the corridor he'd just left and he could watch for a chance to escape.

The first of Stassen's men appeared in the corridor above him about ten minutes after the last explosion. They came cautiously, peering down the darkened tunnel where Daniel was hidden, but spending most of their attention on the lighted corridor and its many doorways. Stassen himself soon appeared and Daniel watched as he organized a systematic search of the upper corridor. One man was left at the tunnel and he was equipped with a powerful light, which he kept trained down the tunnel.

Daniel kept back out of sight and tried to think of a way to get by the man and up the tunnel to the surface. He could shoot and kill him from here, but that would alert the others and he couldn't kill them all. He had to get the man to come down the tunnel.

Daniel thought for several minutes, then began taking off his boots. All of the clothes he'd taken from the lieutenant were similar to those that Stassen's other men wore. Daniel was going to make use of that fact now and in the future.

After taking his boots off, he stripped off his pants and shirt. He put the boots, pants, and shirt in order and arranged them at the back of the tunnel, just around the corner from where the light shone. He tucked the pants legs into the boots, and the shirt into the top of the pants. He stretched out the arms of the shirt, one along the floor of the tunnel, one reaching up the wall of the tunnel and tucked into a crack so it would stay put. When this was finished, he wrinkled the shirt and pants into ghastly lumps and twists.

Now he took some deep breaths, checked to make sure Derl was out of the way and quiet, and prayed a little.

"Say, look at this!" he blurted out in a high, piping voice.

He peeked around the corner to see the effect of his echoing words. The man guarding the tunnel was on his feet, listening intently.

"Where do you think this tunnel leads?" Daniel asked in a deep voice.

"Don't know," high voice replied. "Maybe we should go back?"

"Is that you? Danford? Ivanson?"

Daniel peeked and saw that the guard not only was calling out questions, he also was coming forward with the light in his hands.

"What was that?" high voice squeaked. "Is someone else in this tunnel?"

"Take it easy," deep voice grumbled. "Let's go up a ways and see where the noise is coming from."

Daniel scuffled and beat some rocks against the floor of the tunnel, trying to make it sound like a couple of clumsy spacemen climbing upward.

"Hey, you guys," the guard called. "It's me, Kelly."

"Kelly?" high voice asked. "Is that you, Kelly? Where are you? Can't see a thing in here."

"Stop talking and keep climbing," deep voice ordered.

Daniel stood with his back against the wall. The light was flashing against the wall and coming closer. It was brighter in the tunnel and he could see the clothing he had layed out in the reflections from the walls. Almost time now. He waited.

"What is that?" high voice cried anxiously.

"Stop the thing," deep voice ordered. "Kill it."

"I'm trying," high voice cried. "Oh no. Oh no. What's happening to us?"

"Danford? What's wrong?" the guard, Kelly, called out.

Daniel could see the light jumping now. He could hear feet running, coming closer.

"Oh! God help us!" high voice screamed. "Kelly! Kelly! Aahhh!" Daniel screamed as loud as he could, hoping it wouldn't carry all the way to the men down the corridor. The echoes flew back at him in a chilling cry.

The light bounced around the corner. It struck the upturned boots and swept along the twisted legs and thrown-out torso. Kelly stopped in his tracks. "I'm going to be sick," he whispered to himself. Then he turned to run, fumbling for the radio at his side.

Daniel stepped out, ran a few strides, then struck down on the back of Kelly's neck. The man dropped to the ground without a sound.

Daniel grabbed his feet and dragged him around the corner where he would be out of sight. Daniel quickly threw on his clothes and laced his boots. He picked up Derl, adjusted her weight carefully on his shoulder, and began to run up the tunnel toward the light. He reached the corridor and glanced down it. There were several men in it walking toward him, but they were too far away to see him clearly in the dim light. He didn't pause, just continued on up the tunnel and breathed a sigh of relief when he rounded its first turn.

Here was where the tunnel had been blocked before with a great cement plug. A light was hanging from a crack in the ceiling, but nobody was there. A hole about two and a half feet across had been blasted in the cement. He looked into it and saw light at the other end. There was a mat of some kind laid on the floor of the tiny tunnel, and Daniel immediately saw what it was for.

He lowered Derl to the ground, lashed a cord around her wrists, and looped this around his neck and back to her wrists again. He pushed his head into the small opening and reached out with both hands. He kept his back on the mat and by pulling with his hands and pushing with his legs he was able to propel himself rapidly forward. Derl's arms rested on his stomach and her body slid along the mat between his pushing legs.

The tiny space seemed to go on forever, but soon Daniel was through it and stumbling among the rubble and broken cement that had been cleaned out of the bore hole.

Daniel got to his feet and carried Derl clear. Another bright light was hanging from the ceiling, but it showed nothing but more empty tunnel. Daniel began to run again, carrying Derl. The tunnel turned twice more before he saw light of the sun. He paused, gasping for breath. The last fifty feet he walked, regaining composure and regular breathing. A sentry was sitting in the dirt and brush at the tunnel opening. The bright sunlight blinded him to the darkness of the tunnel and he scarcely glanced at Daniel as he emerged.

"Another live one?" the sentry asked. "First one you've found down below, isn't it?"

Daniel buried his face against Derl's side and kept the girl between them. "Weighs a lot," Daniel grumbled, and began to follow the clearly marked path of muddy footprints and broken brush. It must have rained recently.

"We're keeping them in the Broadway Barracks now," the sentry called after him. "You ought to give them a call before you get there."

Daniel waved his free hand in thanks for the advice, without turning around. When he was among the buildings of the town, he turned off the trail from "Broadway Barracks" to the tunnel, and jogged up a side street. He was tired, but he kept going until he was in the brush at the west edge of the city. Here he sank to the ground, began to take deep breaths, and felt his pulse. He waited until the steady hammering subsided and then he began to consider what to do next.

Derl slowly became conscious of movement. She was sliding, her arms stretched out and pulling her. It was dark and smelled of powdered rock. She was completely relaxed and enjoyed a floating sensation, watching, moving, without effort on her part. She closed her eyes again and felt herself being lifted and carried, her weight resting on her middle and her head hanging down.

It was almost like a dream and in it she also saw lights coming and going—people she could touch if she reached out. But she was too comfortable, or groggy, or lazy. It didn't seem to matter at first—just something disconnected from her.

She opened her eyes again—halfway, then wider. The ground moved by, and feet—heels—lifted and went down again. Her arms swung below her, loosely wrapped by a cord. She moved her fingers, then began to remember.

She closed her eyes tight. Why did dreams sometimes seem better than what really was? She wanted to go back, become disconnected again, but then she changed her mind. It was better to think—and she began to smile. Being enemies. She inspected it carefully, like an egg about to hatch. She touched and poked it. It had brown spots. She wrinkled her nose and pushed it away.

Then she felt herself put on wet ground and realized a lot of time had gone by while she looked at the egg. Something wet dripped on her face and she opened her eyes.

Daniel let a few drops fall on her face, then he set the newly filled canteen on the ground and waited. He watched as her eyes flickered open and was surprised when he didn't see the challenge or the hatred he had expected. Instead he sensed a kind of veiled expression, with reality hiding somewhere within.

She sat up and looked around at the weeds and the brush. Her hand touched the soft ground and she looked at the top of a ruined building she could see in the distance.

"Hello," she said, in a curious, detached way. She looked pale and he involuntarily touched her forehead and felt that it was hot.

"Is something wrong?" he asked. Her neck flushed and then became pale again.

"I don't feel very good," she said and Daniel began to remember what she had gone through in the past several days. He had not helped much by hitting and half suffocating her. Her eyes wandered all around, then she closed and rubbed them.

Daniel offered her a drink, and Derl took the canteen and raised it high as she swallowed rapidly. She set it down, half empty, but it didn't seem to help. She looked at Daniel with a puzzled expression. She had never been sick in her life and she didn't understand the feeling of her stomach. She was thirsty and wanted to drink more, but her stomach felt full and wanted to burst. It was painful and she looked down and wanted to touch and accuse her stomach of tricking her. Then she began to feel really sick.

Daniel watched helplessly as she struggled to her knees and then began to violently reject the water she had just drunk. As she finished, Daniel felt a wrench inside. There were dark splotches of red on the grass. Derl spat a few times, pure blood, then lay back in exhaustion.

Daniel could not take his eyes off the evidence that something was terribly wrong inside of her. For the first time in his life he reproached himself for the physical action he had taken against someone else—although he knew nothing he had done could have caused her internal bleeding. It was just that he was shocked. She had been through so much and had always seemed to him as something indestructible. Now she might be dying and there was nothing he could do personally to help her.

Derl was relaxed and breathing evenly. She watched him with sleepy, half-closed eyes. "I feel a lot better," she said.

Daniel lifted her in his arms and began to carry her back into the ruined city. He would take her to the only place that might offer some help, and that was "Broadway Barracks" and the men he had hoped to escape.

Chapter 25.

The second floor of "Broadway Barracks" was thick with the dust of ages. Daniel waited patiently at the door of the room where Derl had been taken. The closest thing to a doctor among Stassen's eighteen men was in attendance behind the makeshift curtain that hung across the opening in the place of a door.

Darkness was falling outside and it hid some of the decay from sight. Much of the debris on the floor was from plastic that had crumbled and fallen from the roof and walls. Only the formed concrete of the actual floor and walls themselves remained in good condition. Also, surprisingly, the glass in most of the second-story windows was unbroken, and these kept out the wind and the cold.

Daniel and Derl were more fortunate than most of the people Stassen and his men had found hiding in and around the city. These others were confined on the ground floor.

Robert Stassen climbed a set of stairs and entered the room where Daniel was waiting. Stassen sat at a steel desk, on a steel chair, and looked at his newest and potentially most valuable source of information. Every other person discovered wandering about or hiding in the city seemed to be suffering from some kind of shock, or disorientation, which made their memories either blank or confused beyond usefulness.

Daniel spoke first. "You haven't tried to have me disarmed." He said this as both a statement and a question.

"Ah," Stassen said, trying to relax from the work of the day. "'The wicked flee . . .' You're a free man, Daniel Trevor. A citizen of Beta Colony, or, in a wider sense, Earth. Perhaps this is a legalistic excuse to you, but we who live by the rules often abide by them." There was a sparkle of sardonic humor in his eyes as he spoke.

"I'm interested, though," Stassen continued, "in just why you gave Kelly a lump on the head. We are all loaded with recording equipment, and I've seen the films of how you did it, but I'm still interested in the why."

I'll bet you are, Daniel thought, *and you'll never know, if you are lucky.* "It was a simple case of greed," Daniel said. He fingered the shirt he was wearing.

"Yes," Stassen said. "Lieutenant Greely's shirt. I noticed that, and the rest of his uniform. Did you think we would want it back?"

Daniel stepped carefully among the possible traps in Stassen's question. "At first, I just wanted to avoid whoever was blasting into the complex. After I saw who it was, I wanted to avoid complications."

Stassen pointed to the blood and the bullethole in the shirt Daniel was wearing. "Like questions about how those happened?"

Daniel nodded in agreement.

"Well, we know how it happened, so you needn't worry. Still—I don't believe for a minute that those are your real reasons for trying to avoid us." Stassen shrugged. "But they sound good enough to be true so I'll have to be satisfied.

"What about this girl? You've never been attached to anything in your life, unless it was some kind of a killing instrument. So what are you doing trying to take care of her?"

Is that really what she is to me? Daniel thought. He did not answer the question aloud. He was too busy searching for the truth of it. A killing instrument? It sounded cold. "You don't think much of me, do you?" he asked, looking at Stassen.

"Not much," Stassen agreed, "but your personal problems aren't my concern. What I really want to know about is this underground city. What is it? Who made it run? Why is it empty now?"

Daniel watched Stassen for a moment, weighing the questions, smiling at the irony of it all. "I'm going to tell you. Everything. But you know, it's not going to make a damn bit of difference. Even when you know it's the truth."

Stassen said, "Everything we do and hear down here is being sent and recorded on the colony ship. It will be studied and analyzed by experts when they reach Trent. Certainly it will make a difference."

Daniel leaned forward, intent. "But they won't be feeling, living through it firsthand. In a hundred, even fifty years of your report, the words I am saying right now will just be a curiosity, something quaint that *might* have happened when Earth was being resettled."

Stassen did not argue with these remarks, he simply recorded them with all the rest.

Daniel told all he knew of the Nuuian complex and how it operated and what the mines were like. He did not, however, mention anything about Derl, except that they had escaped together from the mine.

Stassen was particularly interested in Daniel's description of the cell chambers and the workings of the mine. And the rings.

"But why coal?" Stassen asked. "Why conquer a world just to steal coal?"

"Perhaps it was the only thing they could transport through their rings. We'll probably never know. But I think it was more than coal. I think it was the conquering that they really enjoyed."

Stassen passed over this speculation. "How did they control all of those workers? A combination of drugs and mind control?"

"Yes."

"You know," Stassen said when they'd finished, "I think I understand better what you said at the beginning. I've seen this underground system. We found the body you mentioned. All of this; the blank people in the room below us, and I can believe it. But just the films, and the words? It makes me wonder."

Daniel could not suppress a tired smile. He was thinking of the people living in the hills and mountains around this very city. With their dogs and testing of children, they would remember a long time after civilization and all the scientists on Trent had dismissed their curiosity and early fears. The Nuuians, if they ever existed, were gone now. Their rumored powers were also gone—and scientists quickly lost interest in something they couldn't hold in their hands.

"Well," Stassen said, standing, "at least I've got a coherent picture of what's been happening here. Beta Colony and the immigration problem should work fine now."

"Yes," Daniel answered, but he wasn't thinking of Stassen's problems or potential triumphs. Daniel was worrying about Derl. Several times during his long talk with Stassen he'd seen the medical officer leave and return carrying trays of covered equipment. Each time the medical officer passed, he would nod and smile with a noncommittal expression.

Daniel stood up and began to pace.

Stassen stood up also and he pointed to the floor. "That, I'm afraid, will have to be your bed for tonight. We haven't mats or blan-

kets enough for our own purposes, let alone the people we are trying to take care of down below."

"I understand," Daniel said. He watched as Stassen left and went
down the stairs.

The medical officer emerged carrying a small medical bag. He was
obviously leaving for the night also.

Daniel stopped him. "What's wrong with her?" he asked.

The officer looked at him curiously. "It looks as if she has been
tortured, or at least starved for several days."

"Yes, I know that," Daniel said impatiently.

The medical officer lifted an eyebrow at this statement and waited
a moment, hoping for some further explanation. But when Daniel
said nothing more, he shrugged. He spoke to Daniel crisply. "From
the description you gave me of the first bleeding episode, I felt it
might be an ulcer of some kind, but fortunately this is not the case.
She was suffering from near starvation and acute dehydration. Her
blood salt was also very low. This is why she was both thirsty and at
the same time couldn't keep any water down. Her blood couldn't be
diluted any further. I gave her a little salt and this allowed her to
take on water and raised her blood pressure to an acceptable level."

"But what about the bleeding?" Daniel asked.

"Yes," the officer said, still watching Daniel with open curiosity.
"She bit her tongue, either purposely, or as a result of the way you
were carrying her. She must have swallowed a lot of it, probably because of the salty taste. Nothing seriously wrong with her. At least
she seems to have her wits about her, which is more than I can say
for the rest of them down on the first floor."

"You talked to her?"

"Not much," the officer said. "Mostly I just brought her food and
stayed to make sure she didn't eat too fast. We spent most of our
time together listening to what you and Stassen were talking about.
She seemed very alert and interested."

The medical officer pushed aside the door-curtain, and Daniel
looked in. Derl was in a makeshift bed, sitting with her back against
the wall. She was chewing on something and looking back at him.

The officer left, but Daniel hardly noticed. He watched Derl and
under his hard gaze she slowly stopped chewing and swallowed. Had
she deliberately forced him to bring her here, where she could gain
control, or had it simply been chance? At any time she could have
one of Stassen's men do away with him. But she hadn't done it yet.

As he stood in the doorway her eyes seemed to search him, hunting for something. Neither of them spoke.

Finally Daniel turned away and closed the curtain. He cleared a space on the floor next to a wall and curled up there and went to sleep. He hardly noticed that the ground was hard.

The medical officer stepped into a room that was dimly lit by a single lamp. Stassen's face was illuminated and he turned to look as the officer closed the steel door behind him. It was one of the few doors that remained intact in the building.

"Well?" Stassen asked. "Anything?"

"No. Not in words, exactly. The girl didn't say anything."

The medical officer sat down. He was obviously trying to formulate something into words, and Stassen waited.

"You know I'm not a fanciful man?" the officer asked.

"Just say it," Stassen ordered. "I'm not the one we're trying to convince, anyway."

"Well—" the officer began, then hesitated. "I swear, when they looked at each other—I could feel it. I mean it. It was something physical—like being on the top of a hill just before lightning strikes. I swear, the hair on my neck stood out just like that, but it was different. I can hardly explain. My arms and legs tingled."

Stassen sat forward, watching intently.

The medical officer shook himself, trying to throw off the symptoms that merely remembering brought him. "It's not something that can be described," he said finally. "The tapes and films aren't going to show a thing."

Stassen sat back, slightly disappointed, but still waiting.

"It started me thinking," the officer continued. "That body we examined down there—I took sweepings off the floor of the cell where we found it." He produced a plastic bag and dumped the contents on the table under the light. "Look at those black threads and the human hairs. That girl was in that cell for a long time before the alien went into it. And another thing: I couldn't find a reason why it died."

"What are you suggesting?" Stassen inquired. Then he held up his hand to stop the officer from interrupting his thought. "You're right! I'll bet you're right. It explains why he tried to get past us."

The medical officer gathered up the bits of material he'd scattered on the table. After he'd returned them to the plastic bag he looked at

Stassen. "Perhaps it would have been better for us if he had gotten past us."

I can't help it. I can't help it. Derl tossed in her sleep. She spoke in her dreams. *Why? Why?* But no answer came. Only echoes and Daniel's cold eyes—like a cliff of steel. She rushed upon it in waves, but broke and drained away. She could find no breaks in the cliff and nothing to cling to.

She was exhausted and seemed to float in the water, effortlessly. Dim lights bobbed in the water below her, like eyes and fish. They watched and called up to her. *What shall we do? Show us.* They had cold greedy voices. The water was cold. She wanted to swim away, but there was nowhere to go. *Help us. Show us. Take us.* The eyes and lights swam closer. They wanted her to eat them, or they wanted to eat her. She couldn't tell.

I don't want to. She tried to go higher in the water, to get away. But the only dry land was a cliff she couldn't scale.

She woke up, sweating. It was dark and she could smell the dust and cold air. She kicked off the cover of her bed and saw a dull flash of reflection from the new plastic cast that the medical officer had painted onto her leg.

The dream was gone, but she didn't try to go back to sleep. She let the cold air of the room touch her legs and wake her up more. She stood up and walked to the curtained door and pushed it back. Daniel was sleeping, curled up on the ground. She wanted to go toward him, but didn't.

I wanted you to help. I tried to call, but you wouldn't answer.

She slipped along the wall and down the stairs. Her feet felt like lifeless wood touching on the stone as she passed. She felt as if she were dragging herself through mud and thick bushes.

The big emptiness of the ground floor surrounded her as she walked slowly toward the open doors. She was actually making it. She kept her eyes on the door, not looking down. But something touched her foot and tried to stop her. She pulled away, but looked down at it. The bearded man's eyes pleaded with her, his arm stretched out to reach her again. She pulled back and stumbled away. But as she did she saw the other eyes. All the eyes in the room were open and they looked at her, begging.

Don't go. Please don't. Take us. Control us.

She fell back through the open doorway. It took all her strength to stand up again. She took a step onto the smooth glass of the street, then fell again. She lay still for a moment on the cold glass. Cold and smooth. It reminded her of her dream.

She turned over and began to crawl slowly down the street. When she could, she stood up and began to walk. Then she stopped and faced back. She brushed the dust and dirt from her arms and knees where she had crawled. She felt proud.

"I can walk," she said aloud. "I don't have to run."

She felt like jumping up and down and shouting. But she didn't, and then smiled at herself for the reason. So much happiness and relief would mean that she really had been scared.

She laughed and didn't feel quite so puffed up. Being scared was O.K. as long as you didn't run *too* fast.

Chapter 26.

The night was dark and moonless, but enough light came from a bright streak of stars for Derl to see a little. She stayed on the glass road and walked slowly. She watched the outlines of buildings against the sky. It was the only way she could measure her progress. A fat short shape between two tall ones. She saw this pattern and made it her next target. She counted steps. There were three hundred twenty before the first tall building was at her shoulder.

The cold of the glass against her feet was funny, because it didn't come into her the way other cold things did. Cold metal came fast and cold rocks slower, but the cold glass was just like a touch of air: cold for a second—then it didn't move anymore. She stopped and smiled. The heat from the bottoms of her feet made the glass warm and comfortable.

She started again and moved closer to the bulk of the fat building. It wasn't tall, but she could almost feel the comfortable fatness of it.

Something reached and grabbed her into the shadow of the fat building. An arm circled under her ribs and another held her mouth. She tried to struggle, but she knew it was Daniel and she couldn't help what happened. She got weak instead of struggling and kicking.

"Did you call me?" Daniel asked, turning her head so she could look at him. "I thought I heard something, but you were gone when I woke up. What were you doing crawling in the street?"

Her eyes were big in the darkness and they just looked at him. She didn't answer because he was holding his hand over her mouth.

As he held her, Daniel could feel the bulge in her stomach. She was like an animal that had eaten too much. She continued to stare at him. He let her go and she almost fell down.

He held her up by an arm. "What's wrong with you?" he whispered. Her eyes couldn't seem to do anything but look at him, big—as if he had killed her.

"Please let go," she asked. "I can't stand up anymore."

He released her and she sat on the road no longer looking at him.
Derl tried desperately to think but nothing happened and she
seemed to be filled up with blankness. Her arms were so weak she
could hardly hold herself in a sitting position. She couldn't help it.
Being this close to him was like falling into a well. She was alive because he'd got near to her and made her fall back into her body.
She'd been trapped in that underground cell, trying to find a way
out. But the holes in the walls were too small and he'd come in the
door and she couldn't get by. Now he was making her weak again
and he didn't even know it. She tried to breathe deeply and feel the
glass of the road. This helped and she could blink her eyes and think
a little.

Daniel could see that she was looking at him again and that there
was a change in the expression—something more normal. He knelt,
not knowing exactly what to say. He didn't want to start her fighting
again, but he didn't know any other way of thinking. He'd never been
a friend or tried to have a friend. Not for a long time.

"I—" He stopped, trying to think of something better to say. "You
could have killed me any time in there—any of those people on the
first floor could have done it for you. You can go back now, if you
want. I just followed you to—" He stopped before he could lie. "I
was going to take you again by force, if I had to. If you don't go
back soon I—I still will do it." He didn't go any further for fear he
would change his mind on the spot.

Derl pushed away from him with her feet, sliding backward on the
smooth glass. She stood up and brushed at the invisible dust on her
legs.

Daniel forced himself to stay where he was.

She watched him struggling with himself, wanting to get up and
force her to stay with him again. There was still something in the
glance between them, some barrier that he wouldn't let go of. She
wanted it to go away, but knew it might never do that.

She turned and began to walk, passing away from the fat building
and toward the second of the skinny ones.

Daniel followed, still uncertain as to what he would have done if
she had turned back and tried to go the other way.

Daniel led the way. What little they had in the way of provisions
he carried on his back. Derl followed, limping slightly. Her face
reflected conflicting thoughts, but she stepped lightly and kept up

without complaint. Her eyes were a little lost as she tried to fix upon
a solution to some problem she wrestled with inside.

Neither spoke and the city and road were far behind them now.
The sun was up and trying to dry the wet grass of a small meadow
they were crossing. It was here that Derl decided that things could
not stay the same anymore. She was angry that she could not form
the words that would break what he was holding between them.

She stooped to the ground suddenly and picked up several pebbles. She flung one at the back of Daniel's head and another at his
leg. Both were well aimed.

Daniel turned, surprised, then angry at the sharp pain. He ducked
quickly as a third stone passed his ear. He stepped closer, intent on
putting a stop to it.

She swung at him, unexpectedly, striking his neck with a fist gripping pebbles. He started to swing in return, but changed the motion
and grabbed at her shoulder instead. She ducked, butting him in the
chest, stepping on his toe, trying to trip him.

All he could think was that she had gone crazy.

They fell together and he tried to avoid landing on her splinted
leg, with which she was kicking him.

Then he knew what was happening.

She was under him and the tension in her body was changing. The
squirming and punching stopped. She tried to press up against him.
Her heart was pounding, little breasts were sharp against him. Puffs of
hot breath burned his neck.

"I hate you!" she cried with all her heart.

"You—" He wanted to hit her and rape her and hurt her for the
trick she was trying to play on him. But he couldn't and her eyes
changed and became frightened. Her heart pounded and her eyes
stung and filled with water. They were trying to tell him and asking
and asking and asking. The same question he would never answer.

Daniel felt something change in his mind. He looked at Derl and
for the first time he knew he wasn't afraid.

He could feel her small body, all of it beating with fear, and her
eyes, helpless, risking everything, trying somehow to help.

She became, somehow, suddenly real—a part of the universe that
was really and truly not subject to his will. And this was so precious
—even if only to have in opposition.

He saw flecks of brown and gold in her eyes and knew that it was
surely the first time he had ever looked into them. He lowered his

head to her shoulder and crushed her to him, gently, for just a moment. Then he let her go and sat back. He felt a little dizzy at the change in the tension between them.

He looked at her, touching the black parachute silk covering her legs. "Someday," he said, "when you're more than bones and elbows, you may succeed and really seduce me."

Her face spread with a bashful smile. She felt strangely flushed and frightened at something that had become, for her, almost a fate. She was sitting up, and she took his hand and held it in her own. She pulled it open and held it palm up in front of her. Then she put her own fist inside it and let three warm pebbles drop out. She closed his fingers around the little rocks, which were almost hot from her touch.

"You keep these," she said and closed her eyes to relish the pleasure.

Daniel watched as Derl brought the last of the wood for the fire—mostly branches and broken twigs. She dumped them on the ground and brushed at the few that clung to her clothing. She stepped around the sharp rock of the ledge in her bare feet, then sat down and waited for him to tell her what else to do. The plastic cast on her lower leg flashed from the light of the lowering sun.

He had chosen the ledge because it was protected above and below by rocky slopes difficult for animals to climb, but easy enough for him and Derl. It had other advantages too. A streak of white rock cut across the face of the mountain, and where it intersected the ledge, its underside had rotted away to form a little cave. Trees below were high enough to block it from view, but by climbing the bare rocks a little higher up, he could see the valley with the road and river, and far away, the outlines of the city. A little higher still was a notch in the ridge, and through this, if need be, they could escape into another network of streams and valleys.

He took a small ball of fishing line from his pack and handed it to Derl. "There is a hook wrapped in the center of that," he told her. "See if you can go down and catch some fish. Don't go below the place where the boulders make a waterfall."

She took the ball in her hand and wrapped her fingers around it. He watched as she picked her way along the ledge and onto the trail that led down to smooth ground. She limped only when the foot of her splinted leg stepped on something sharp. The skin on the bottom of that foot had become tender from lack of use.

Daniel turned back and began to finish the work he had begun at the mouth of the cave. He was using large rocks, dead wood, and the limbs of a fallen pine to narrow the opening of the cave and close it off from the wind. He wanted to make it good enough to stay the winter. Stassen had told him of the coming weather and he wanted to stay close enough to the city. There were sure to be materials in the abandoned buildings that he would find useful. And Stassen had mentioned that he would be leaving the city and returning to island site, taking the dazed refugees with him. Daniel smiled as he worked. Surely the island colony would be a complete success now that Stassen was going to run it personally.

Daniel stopped his work and looked down the slope into the trees below. The forest was so quiet he could hear faint splashing sounds and something like a patternless humming broken by laughter. Daniel listened. He suddenly felt that it was vitally important that he explain to himself and to her the change that had made it possible for her to laugh and for him to listen to laughter.

The ground near the cold stream was nearly level and soft, so he could walk without making any noise. She was quiet now and he found her by following tracks in the soft ground. He saw her and stopped. She seemed to be asleep, lying in a patch of grass. Her feet were crossed and propped up on a rock near the water. He could see that the fishing line came from the water, threaded between toes and crossed knees. It was tied to her right wrist, which flopped on her stomach. Several fish lay in the grass next to her, wriggling.

As he stepped closer she opened her eyes, looking contented. She scratched her shoulders against the ground by moving gracefully, then she closed her eyes again. Before he could speak she said, "Fish are easy. They are always hungry."

Daniel walked around and sat down next to her on the side away from the fish she had caught. He could feel the pebbles she had given him, in one of the buttoned pockets of his shirt. He could feel their rounded shapes against his skin.

"I've always felt that men and women were basically different," he said.

She sat up and looked at him. Her eyes were always big when she watched like that, and Daniel continued.

"There is something in a man that makes him want to do a great thing, go somewhere, find something. I don't know exactly how to say it, but I know it's there. I saw how it could make a man eager to get up in the morning and look at things as if they were really new and he could do what was needed. But I saw it all die, too, and a woman was always there to say it was impossible, or that someone had already done it, or who cares?—we've got to eat.

"I swore it wouldn't happen to me—that nothing would change what I am or what I'm really trying to do."

Derl was looking at him, but her eyes had become unfocused. She was listening so hard that parts of her skin seemed to tingle.

"I think I hated you," Daniel continued. "I was afraid. I was afraid that you could reach up and take hold of some part of me that no one else could reach."

Derl's head jerked a little, as if it were trying to lift from her shoulders. She wanted to say something. But she felt frozen, fixed by his words, which were somehow terrible—but at the same time she accepted them and was surrounded by them. They were a part of what he was and she could almost feel the fear of what he was trying to explain in herself.

"I almost killed you," he said. "The first time I saw how you might become valuable to me—I almost killed you. I was afraid that if I tried to carry anything with me, or even held on to something, that I would lose everything—all the sureness and certainty that I've always had."

Daniel's eyes seemed to waver as he tried to look at all of Derl and make her understand.

"You can't know what it is like," he said, "when you're alone and all you can see are hands that are trying to reach out to pluck you down and away from what you are trying to be."

Derl couldn't help herself. She fell forward and lay against Daniel's chest. Her mind swam with the vision of how she had almost drowned—of all the hands reaching for her and demanding. She couldn't understand how she and Daniel could reach for each other and not be hurt, but she knew it could be that way.

How could reaching in some ways be so good, and in others so bad?

She couldn't say all this in words but somehow she tried to say it by holding on to him. She couldn't help that she cried and was too weak to do anything else but hold on.

Daniel could not form the words to explain why he had stopped being afraid of her. It had happened.

She stopped crying and he touched her shoulder. She let go of him   K1 and took his hand off her shoulder and held it between both of hers. They were cold and trembled slightly.

"Sometimes it makes me weak and I cry when you're trying to be so honest."

Daniel smiled a little sadly, remembering the last time he had been honest and brutal and made her cry.

She seemed to recover suddenly and turned away from him, pointing at the shining plastic of her cast. "The doctor said I could take it off in a month, just by heating it over a fire, then putting it in cold water. It just crumbles away."

Daniel looked at the cast. He'd seen them before and knew that they just crumbled away. But to Derl it was marvelous and he laughed at the serious way she was looking at him.

"Yes. It just crumbles away."